LOST STORIES FOUND

LOST STORIES FOUND

ALAN R. MARTIN

CONTENTS

House of Games...3

A Prince and His Dark Kingdom 23

The Forgotten Incident..............................31

Sudden Chillness......................................41

A Dark Moment.......................................55

On The Wall..63

A Stranger In A Saloon..............................71

A Winter Coldness Appears........................89

An Innocent Man....................................105

A Brief of the story

In this story you will read about a 'Queen's' rule in the year 1326. This is about a Queen and her cunning ways to get what she wants. There is a short paragraph to describe the 'Queens' character. The "cunningness... cleverness... of her majesty" with her, moody heartless inconceivable tantrums and her conniving ways, had those around her, very suspicious of the state of mind she was in. Some thought she simple was "crazy or even mad... stark raving mad!" The story is called: *House of Games.*

HOUSE OF GAMES

An unnatural tumultuous of screams had appeared, shouting out with fears from the past. The gathering of antiquated merchandise was being presented. But one would look at the other, what use are these, for these are subject to the heaves of someone's congestion. The crowd was determined to get what they came for, asking where the delight was, to fill one's anger. What was the judge and the mayor, and the members of their families done with the promise of the feast and the provisions that the Governor has offered?

His subjects were jesting to King Tobias, about the feast, the year was 1326; what shall we tell them, for this time the crowd looks frightening, and their demands will not be shrugged off as we had successfully done last time. The 'King signaled' to his henchmen to 'inquire about the Queen,' she will inform you of what to do next. She's been running the parlor games setting up the rules and the instructions of how to play. As they approached her majesty while she was wearing her white length gown, adorned from her shoulders down to the outstretched floor and the sparkling of her jewels gleaming their exquisite rays from beyond her neck, the squires that came to forewarn her and said, the villagers are at it again.

"Queen Zephyr," nodded to the servant who brought the message replying what will become of them, --- 'without me.' She smiled ever so smugly...

The leisurely quaintness that the Queen preceded, announced to the citizens from her balcony inquiring them, have patience you will be attended too. The steadiness and calmness of her voice brought the crowd to silence, 'moving on her every word.' With her presumptuous smile and her delicate charm, she delighted the crowd promising, that things will change and there will be food and parcels to acquire and to partake... I will give you my divine oath and attention that there will be preservation for your livelihood.

The eloquence of her soft- smooth tone had the crowd eating out of her hands. The shouting, the jeering, the echoing started cheering, 'long lives the Queen,'... 'long lives the Queen'.... She would put her hands in the air gesturing to her subjects, 'her thoughtfulness,' her kindness, a symbol of symbolic trust and worthiness.

Then 'she would calmly announce,' be off and wait for tomorrow and there will be a banquet, a festival beyond one's imagination beginning on the fourth- hour, so come back then.

This was an elegance of hegemony, this official dominance in power, the leadership of the land, the only place to acquire the spoils needed for a day's ration that they knew of. The poor peasants from the village had been satisfied with the "Queens' 'admonishment, for she had advised to come back at a certain hour and there will be a joyous occasion to proclaim.

While the last of them eventually turned to walk back to their miserable life living in a town of slum and broken-down abodes, there, was still some complaining of where they, under their tongues showed loudness of their voice, for they barely had roofs with rotted out rooms of heated stench, as the sun kept parching it's burnt- out waves amongst the villagers.

Their condition was a place of unbar-ability, then to add to their suffering the ground was so dry and hard you could not even turn the sod over with a pointed spike or blade. Not to mention growing any crop that would take and grow in the spoils of this soil for it was beyond its usefulness, but the pungent stiffness of different stagnant of weeds were flourishing with such exemplifying wonderment.

For all the stock and livelihood that the villagers had; had been required by the King and his henchmen, they subdued the peasants by enforcing taxes, and when that was exhausted, they merely pilfered the rest from other forms needed to "indulge the Queen." They have become reduced to starving peasants that the King has conquered.

The water was rationed one – skin pouch per person, per day. But as the townspeople have become mistreated, malnourished, and misconstrued they have become wiser.

They would whisper amongst them-selves an allegiance of conspiracy towards the King and his subjects… forming meetings in secrecy to hide from the obstruction of the King and his palace relatives! In desperation their planning, their actions, their very intentions will need to be forthright a calculated risk that will 'end inn murder…!'

Their thoughts have summed up the conclusion without a King, there will not be any use of subjects and internal sabotage renouncements.

A demoralizing salutation was announcing itself in a tight circle. Their attitude has singularly united a bond within one- another.

After languishing and struggling over a period of' two and one – half years being enslaved and in a form of bondage the settlers were orchestrating a plan to do away with the King and his appointed courtiers. Whatever it took, to break the yolk that was hanging about their necks, tired of holding on to the conditions that the poor peasants were living in.

As the peasants in the shambled town were patiently planning their strategy, they remembered the last encounter with the King and his henchmen. For they tried 'six -months back' to overtake the castle and were struck asunder, they sent us, after 'killing twenty' of us. And sent us all in different directions running for our lives. We do not want to repeat our first mistake, not properly planning a good strong strategy! Contemplating their new game – plan required how many of us are willing to fight, and who are willing to die for our freedom.

One of the more noticeable villagers, 'Ignatius spoke up' and responded, we have one-hundred and fifty of us who are willing to abolish the unnecessary cruelty that comes henceforth from the King. They are ready to do what is necessary to capture or even kill the King and his henchmen. But what and how shall we commence in battle; for we do not have the weapons to fight, in hand-to-hand sparring. Well, said one, and his name was 'Sergio a Spaniard amongst them said,' we have started making and acquiring without notice bows and arrows along with sharp stones to make spears, and forging swords in discretion. All these implements are in hiding until the right opportunity presents itself. We still have several days until we can meet the necessary standards before we begin the arrangement.

Who will give the signal when the time to attack is forthright? This is the reason we are here, to determine when would be the right occasion to go and begin the fight, also, how to proceed, having ourselves in the proper positions before the shout of battle starts. But there are some of us inside the castle upon entering in, by deception. Then the "signal of battle will come after the shouting of murder" is heard through the castle doors and windows, and perhaps the towers.

For those who are inside the castle will be killing the kinsmen in secrecies and hiding in the shadows while looking for the King. The rest of the townspeople will be rushing in toward the castle's drawbridge waiting for it to be lowered, and upon entering the fighting will hinge on the few who were in there earlier as a diversion.

'Sydney', another townsman spoke up saying, I have counted one – day of how many men the King that has been summoned to circle and gather; surrounding the castle, and the servants that serve him and his men, and the number was two – hundred and fifty, as I ask again, how will we succeed in this battle? What presumably looks like slaughter! And still another, had a negativity on this gruesome adventure, in his eyes it appeared they were more superior in nature and stature.

Then the one who arranged the meeting stood up and said we have one thing they do not, 'his name was Alexander,' and he said, he stated something unusual, most of them in that half – blown apart barn had shown unequivocal looks on their faces. A shock expression was still on their face when he mentions, "we have right on our side." He repeated himself we have the "God given right on our side" whereas the King with his voluntary kinsmen robbed us and downright shackled us into a form of slavery, as 'Merlin agreed with him' in a tone of acknowledgement.

Now as the peasants in their small beaten downtown were instructing a plan with their fellow man, the King and the palace were having their daily meals served to them in the grandeur banquet room.

* * * * *

The servants were serving cooked hot potted – roast with mashed potatoes and a savory gravy made from the stock of beef. All their provisions were attended by the cooks, servants and gardeners, and overseeing them were the King's kinsmen. The eloquence of pictures of wars and Kings with their 'Queens' in another portrait were sitting on the walls, and crystallized chandeliers were hanging from the arch – ceilings with all its exquisite colors mainly adorned with light – bluish texture reflecting the tint that glowed, brought forth where the dining table was situated.

The oval – shaped windows were elaborated with stained colored glass and setting four- meters apart.

The hard - wood dining tables length was 'nine – meters by 'three – meters in width'. There was enough room to set seventy – five people with servants hustling to bring out the main course of delicacy. It was the "Queen…" who would teach those at the table their manners or she would remind them of the consequences. She would imply, this is the 'Queens and Kings' table and I will have order…! She would allow the events of the day to be discussed and thought upon, as long it was in a civil and courteous style, that it would be acceptable.

When she spoke, there was silence in the halls and rooms to hear her every word, for you didn't want to miss out, because it could be your head if she got angry! This was her castle, her treasure, her gold, her silver and her precious stones. This was her paradise and she made sure you knew it!

They had acreage upon acreage of livestock with gardens and fruit trees that were fenced in from 'so-called' volunteers of the villagers of whom the mayor and or the governor requested. It was reigned in with a tight stern not allowing anybody around or inside without the proper authority giving them permission to enter or examine the quality of their food supply.

They would look upon this as standard procedure, when someone wanted to proceed inside the gates and the high fences that kept things in place. These "crucible metal fences stood fourteen feet in height" and there was a barbed wire running across the top. They would choose the weak peasants to enter the blacksmith shop and stoke the furnaces to bring up the heat, so they could set the ore to calcine, below its melting point. After melting it would collect in the hollow bottom of the ore furnace. Now it was ready to pour into templates that was pe-made for more fences to be tied together and assembled after it was cooled off. This also provided means of forging weapons for his kinsmen and their subjects.

As for water, in the middle of this big, plotted land was an underground-spring that formed a lake with measurements that exceeded 'one – hectometer.' There were trenches formed for any over – flows from the spring, they were diverted to the lower sections to fill up wooden barrels that were placed on carts.

They used oxen to pull the carts, to water down the livestock that were in the pastures of other sections.

Horses were scarce there were only seven left, and they were pampered by the 'Queen.' Only the 'King and Queen' with the two - care takers could ride them by the order and permission of the Queen.

There were 'three – fountains' that spewed water in the air at a distance of '2-meters' and then dropped to settle back in the basin. With different assortments of bushes and berries, while the flowers arrayed on two- sides in this exquisite ground site along this small lake.

The attention from the gardeners kept them refreshed and in beautiful sight, for this is one thing the 'Queen requested' … without any excuses.

The last person who refused to obey the instructions from the 'Queen' is sitting in the dungeon awaiting their verdict. 'Delia,' has been in there for the last three – weeks and the discussion must be waiting for the 'Queen….' To make up her mind!

They have learned earlier do not make haste to the Queen, for she will rule over you with an iron fist! Let her go about her business thinking there isn't a care in the world, so she can play her games, putting everybody on the edge of their seat. Some have wondered if she is somewhat insane or just merely delirious!

The fortress with its heighten towers and domes were at least one third of a hectometer straight into the air. Who could waver over this height?

The saw – tooth top parapet rim with mortars of stone and brick were 'two – half decameters,' sitting and adjoining the four towers. This massive dwelling was fortified to prevent enemies from entering the castle barriers. The castle was built 'four – hundred years ago' and we heard it took, two -thousand strong arm carpenters,' masons, and laborers. The moat that encircled the outer barriers of the castle's structure was six – meters across and was used for the castle's waste slush. This exclusive mansion needed lots of attention to maintain the livelihood that the 'Queen requested.' 'The King took care of the outside business and affairs, while the 'Queen maintained and controlled' the inside as well as the interest that kept her delightfulness.

The King would assume the responsibility of all law – abiding activities and of course the seriousness of the charge may indulge to come forth and set up a hearing.

If the accusations are being disputed with one or more than one – party, then the judge would activate the courts to proclaim a trial is in order.

Depending on the outcome, the 'Queen' still held the trump card, deciding what the defendant's final sentence would incur, and their dilemma.

All those around knew the 'Queen,' she was the one, who would oversee the courts, and 'she had the final decision of the ruling.' 'What the 'King and judge' were merely suggesting was trivial; what was going to happen as they went through the motions and processes, even the defendant's counselor's and lawyers knew the game she played! But they would say to one another, "what shall we do? They all knew you couldn't stand-up and argue with the 'Queen.' The last man that tried, he is now "buried without his head on his shoulders." For the execution was, she had his head sliced using the 'guillotine in the torture room'. "She had it placed outside the walls for all to see!"

As the 'Queen roamed' within the castle walls there was a maiden with her, to serve her every whim.

She would not hesitate at any moment to embark upon the King her desires, her passions, her flamboyant greediness of precious apparel and jewelry that she had requested or plainly downright insisted. For if the promises weren't kept the rage of the 'Queen became unbearable,' when the demands were heard and not received, a dauntless shrewdness would be showing on the 'Queen's face!' The King in turn, treated her with admirable humbleness, letting her run about the castle threatening the servants to please her anguished haughtiness!

All those who were inside the castle stayed away as far as possible, hoping to not run into the 'Queen,' for they all knew what she could do.

'Fear was in the eye's,' of the courtiers, servants and maidens, there was silence throughout the castle rooms, walls and ceilings. She would trample around the fortress with 'blood in her eyes', seeking anyone to bring her punishment to some form of justice. Even the 'King kept his distance,' knowing in his mind there's nothing you could do to keep her at ease!

The "cunningness... cleverness... of her majesty" with her, moody heartless inconceivable tantrums and her conniving ways, had those around her, very suspicious of the state of mind she was in! Some thought she simply was "crazy or even mad... stark raving mad!"

The temperament of her emotions could change in a heartbeat. Her insidious imagination set the tone of the castle's improbability.

What made this an unusual circumstance was the attribute that the Queen possessed, with the eloquence of her beauty and appearance, for the King and all those that were underneath him, they knew she had the audacious tenacity to keep the peasants and townspeople in harmony and content with her soft - voice.

Echoing promises of banquets, and festivities, and all the parcels and drink to make one merry. The 'Queen knew...' she had them over a barrel, in her mind she had everybody fooled, her quaint dismal allure had all those around to observe her every movement, her reactions, 'her words... yes, her words....' Were the rules of the game that she played in the ...." House of Games....!"

The fourth hour was approaching as the ignorant peasants were straggling in, in small bands standing in front of the drawbridge waiting to see if the 'Queen' would keep her promise.

They dare not to cross the bridge yet fear of the King and his henchmen who would drive them away, 'without the Queen being present.' Her hand maidens spotted the townspeople coming in and forming groups outside of the drawbridge from the windows of her room. And informed the 'Queen,' with your permission may I speak to your majesty? As her hand maiden spoke of the townspeople joining together across the bridge and reminded her of the feast and it is the fourth hour that you have spoken of!

From her 2nd floor balcony, she glanced down at the crowd, and with a half hearten grin on her face, she replied, well…. Let's give them what I promised, and at that time a servant approached, the King has sent me, he tarried so you may have the honor and privilege to do what pleases you.

The Queen jested to the servant, tell the King, I had promised a festival and a banquet so have him set up the necessary fire pits and the fatted hogs to feed these peasants. In her mind this should last another week, for it was a week ago, before they had their last elaborate meal. Her cunning and deceitfulness were why the poor peasants trusted the 'Queen's words.'

There were times when the Queen waited ten- days before feeding the boorish peasants.

The King had the poor peasants along with the servants attending the fire – pits with spindles attached to a U – shape holder to allow rotating of the slab of meat being cooked.

His henchmen would oversee the projected celebration as the 'King' picked out the fatted hogs with which the caretakers would start the butchering process, with the help of the townspeople doing what is commanded of them.

Water was pulled from the springs lake and filled in barrels drawn over by the oxen – carts to the outskirts of the fire – pits. There would be five – carts with four – barrels on each one, as the lines began forming up to get a drink. There would be a servant at each barrel and a dispensing ladle for dispersing. So, they would take turns drinking water, one – ladle per – person. Of course, the ladle would hold about two – gills of water.

The cooks and their subjects were overseers of the five – wooden tables adjoining the fire – pits preparing the banquet that was required from the 'Queen.' 'She gave her word,' there will be a feast and she was looking past the promise of this engagement.

Her thoughts were focused, if I would make merry a short time of celebration and feed these unmentionable peasants that all things will look upon me, as their 'Queen of delightfulness.' She reminded herself this will give me control and power above all!

The partake of the spoils of nourishment has drowned out the anger and cries of women and their children for another week. The men in the village have filled their bellies and their anger has subsided for another day, and the remains of the feast they could take home to enjoy for another occasion. They also left with their skin – pouches full of fresh water, for it was a dark late evening.

Earlier water was distributed in the morning, so during this day they had two rations of water and more.

While the Queen succeeded with her intentions, she leisurely sat on her throne while drinking wine from her chalice – goblet imploring her maid servants, how well the celebration had fared. The 'Queen instructed' to her hand maiden's, fill my chalice one – more time and be off with you, for tomorrow will be another day.

As the 'Queen' was getting her fill of the delightful juices of berries, the King was instructing his henchmen and servants, do the necessary formalities and set the guards in their rightful places. He gave warning to his top henchmen's overseeing his authority's jurisdiction.

And the 'Queen' will decide your fate! They thought amongst them – selves after the King had left, wondering, we have never been threatened by the King using the "Queen as the hammer....!" But they all knew the King had made a serious declaration.

The prominent townspeople with their share of nourishment were in shape for discussion and retribution and decided to set them – selves aside for a new day. They looked upon each other and inquired who could argue at this time for my eyes are getting heavy from the satisfaction of my bodily desires. For I seemed to have been fulfilled! For there was no contestant from others, for there will be another day of contorted misery. The poor peasants in their drab appearance and their uneducated demeanor were simply misinformed of what the 'Queens intentions were!' Or who could predict what the 'Queen would do next!'

At the start of the new day, it was the townspeople holding a secret meeting with others standing guard waiting on the King's kinsmen to show up for the tasks that would be assigned to them. Their short but informed gathering consisted of what means have we've learned? The foremost scheme needed acknowledgement, what would be the plan to deceive the guards and servants to put ten of us in the castle. When this has been accomplished, we can go to stage two or the second step.

The 'game plan consisted,' this would be best, when the sun has gone down, and the darkness of the moon and stars are not to come out at night. The 'gloominess and haziness of mist' from the lake would be the time to enter the castle unannounced. They agreed, and one asked which day can we expect this dreariness to happen? There was one amongst them who studied the sky and he quoted; 'the stars are telling me,' It will be tonight or perhaps tomorrow night!

Now the next phase of entry they question after the murders have been screamed about, who will lower the draw - bridge? The draw - bridge was usually drawn up, when the sun went down.

We need to send two out to lower the bridge when the time is right, while most of us will be waiting with our weapons to destroy and kill with surprise around the castle's outer walls.

We will first surround the rooms of the servants, the cooks, gardener's, with other labors' peasants and kill them in their housing quarters as quietly as we can. This should give us the element of confusion when 'suddenly the hollers of screams and anguish are crying out in the darkness at night!'

A concern voice from two of the townspeople quarreled with the others and implied, would it not benefit us to attack the guards and henchmen first?

13

For those will be the ones with weapons and we need to take them by surprise! After the plan was laid out, they looked at each other and someone said, "We will work out the final details later, this was when the 'King's henchmen' showed up to gather the peasants for their daily assignments. This is the time in which jobs were selected by the mayor and his subordinates. It was set up and pre- arranged for the day.

As the day fared, the peasants that were working and attending to the services required from the mayor's authority found out where the 'King' was hiding and storing weapons for his henchmen. While his henchmen were opening the door to the tunnel, they got a glimpse of the passage that led to the torture room, and it adjoined the dungeon.

When the sun was beginning to hide behind the setting of the hills, the moment came to fill your skin – pouch with water and head back to the crumbling town for rest and perhaps a new day.

The meeting was quietly being attended in the old half-roof barn that there used to. When all got the word, they came in groups finding a spot to sit while mumbling to each other about the ventures they had endured for the hour. When the conference came to some form of order, was when the more noticeable leader along with the somewhat 'stargazer announced,' and his name was 'Merlin,' it will take place after midnight, and we shall start entering the castle.

There will be twelve of us, two will draw near the draw – bridge, eight of us will be going to capture the towers and overthrow them; kill, if necessary, in secret any obstructions. Any noise could spoil the element of surprise. Two of us will find the King and do away with him! We will go in twos, a pair where one will look out for the other.

While they shared information amongst their-selves midnight was approaching. They all in turn had their weapons, and a plan to adhere, for this they told themselves would be the last stand.

When the draw – bridge falls all pandemonium will break loose inside the castle walls. Kill and murder those who come against you was their advice! It was also told to them the tunnel that led to the torture room is where you can find weapons, but it is guarded.

* * * * *

As they proceeded the twelve managed to get inside the castle and their point of entry was through the tunnel that was mentioned.

They realized there were two guards attending the entrance to the torture chamber. This presented a problem. For they were well equipped with swords and shields. As they thought this out, something strange happened to the henchmen. They were getting bored and started playing a game, to where they were discussing who could win at a certain game. It involved getting on the floor on their knees or sitting down. This game indulged who the better player was. It participated in money, privileges, and tasks, that one who lost would have to take the slack from the other participant. These bets had to take concentration in order to exceed the other contestants.

As they were playing, they had their backs turned from the tunnel entrance. As they were distracted with their games the peasants were creeping against the walls with their torn-up clothes and it was blending in with the grayish rocks, stones and concrete. They proceeded slowly and had their spears ready to pierce them in the back when they got close enough. The guards had a metal sheath on the front chest side of their abdomen.

When they finally reached close enough from both sides of the wall, they gave a silent gesture to each other, and lounged suddenly and jumped quickly from both sides and pierced both in the sides and watched them mumble with a quiet death, as their eyes rolled with dis-belief.

As they roamed through the torture room, they found weapons they could use and left their old ones in a secret area. When they went into the dungeon, they found a girl still behind bars. She said if you help me, I'll help you, besides I have nothing to lose. They had all agreed and said we don't have much time to squander. As they broke off from each other in pairs the woman stayed with the one who was in charge. Delia knew the passages to the upper chambers.

While squirming their way to the four -towers they came across, only to find one guard at each main corridor that led to the chambers on each floor and with trickery and deceiving conjures, they murdered their way up to the towers.

In order to keep the 'noise and screams' from penetrating through the stillness of night, they would cut their throats from behind or drive a sheave in their backs or perhaps a thrust of a spear through the side.

To get to where the look – outs of the towers presumed, you had to climb up a ship's ladder and knock on the hatch that was bolted and latched to the floor of the tower.

If the hatch was down then it would indicate that the tower was occupied and presumably locked, but if it was opened then it would indicate or seem the tower was empty; no – one there. When we approached and glanced up to the deck of the tower, we seen the trapped – door was closed! We looked at each other and thought, what will be our plan? One said, while whispering, let's go up and knock and start an escapade telling the guardsman to open, we need help down here. The other said, but what should we shout about?

We need to involve the King and here's the plan! 'Shout, the King needs help there's intruders on the top floor and we need assistance. Climbing the ladder one of them banged on the trap – door of the hatch furiously shouting 'open – Open up in the King's name, for we are in dire need' – hurry there's no time to waste!

And when the trapped- door was opened, the henchman peered down the rungs of the ladder and seen a spear thrusting him in the throat. The blood from his gurgling voice was starting to squirt in different directions as he fell from the deck onto the bottom floor of the tower. As he was waiting for the next guard to appear, he heard the hatch slamming as the guard was trying to seal himself from the intruder. The peasant lodged his spearhead between the hatch and its frame, not allowing it to close.

They heard shouts and screams from the guard stuck in the tower. Echoing we have intruders from the tower he was in; in a few moments the awakening of the castle brought light and lanterns to see what the commotion was all about!

We whispered to one – another, how are we going to shut him up, he's waking- up the 'whole castle' We shouted to the guard what are you doing? You idiot do you want to wake up the 'Queen.' Now open this hatch before the Queen takes your head and possibly ours too!

The guard stopped and thought about the situation and pondered. Maybe he's right she'll have my head if this turns out to be a false alarm. But if it isn't a false alarm my head will be taken also!

At that moment the 'King,' came in with two of his courtiers and seen the guard had opened the hatch, and his throat was plunged as he was lying on the floor. The second guard was still in the upper deck awaiting instructions.

The 'King screamed' with bloody anger and his voice, shouted to his henchmen,' kill them we have intruders trying to take over the castle. Little be known there were two townspeople behind a wall beside the ladder, at a distance from the "King and his courtiers." And when the second guardsman peered his head from the opened latch a townsman shot him in the neck. He landed while leaning over on the bottom floor. At this time the two peasants climbed the ship's ladder to the top deck of the tower.

The two peasants who killed the guards were stuck inside the tower, and they proceeded to shoot at the King and his henchmen, with bows and arrows, that they had acquired from the guardsmen weapon area in the tunnel of where the torture chamber is located, on the side there lied the torment of the dungeon in the underground cellar of weapons. Here they were isolated within, behind the trapped – door, that they had left open to engage in a duel with the King and his henchmen.

As they looked out upon the windows of the tower they seen the draw – bridge had been lowered to allow the other peasants to fight in battle, their freedom and liberty amongst the henchmen, and other courtiers who engaged in war. Spears and arrows were being thrust to one another in fierce combat against each other. This bloody feud seemed it lasted for hours, but it was over in about 30- minutes. The peasants took over, and they were shouting out howling, this is our hour of control and power.

The battle had officially started and there was no turning back! The two – townsmen that had followed the 'King' and his courtiers were watching behind the wall that led to the tower room bottom-floor.

As the two peasants were stuck in the tower, wondering what they should do next? For they were worried because they were running out of arrows!

As they were spying with all the commotion being addressed; the condition that their fellow friends were in, they found their-selves in an obstructive situation. Being stuck in an attic of no-where to flee. It seemed to bring danger to circumvent and a possible disaster. Then a sadistic thought crossed their mind!

If we do not murder them, disaster will come to us, and we will be killed. Crawling ever so cleverly and cautiously, they got behind the 'King', those'd who were behind in the lower section. Of course, there were only two of them that were watching their brothers in the tower. They were captured in the tower but stuck isolated and into the drains of dormant along the walls behind the King's courtiers as they had their back against them in entrapment.

The two behind the wall on the lower level were crawling ever so cleverly, they got behind the 'King' and one of his nearby henchmen was pierced through their side with a slick sharp edge from a sword and was initially dead in a quiet form. He slit his throat for good measure. Nobody seemed to notice.

The other courtier, after seeing this stood up and ran, but before he got too far an arrow entered below his shoulder blade! So, silence was maintained in this particular; tower of dead bodies, lying about in waste.

The one peasant took the sharpest – slipperiest-edged sword they had and decapitated the 'King's head from his shoulders' and waved it out the window, as there were screaming bloody murder out in the courtyards from battle. He was hanging on his hair.

As he was screaming from the top of his lungs, he was shouting, "Here is your King," come, see. "This your 'King' what do you have to say now"? With the lantern he took the King's head and lit it on fire! Shouting with a loud fiery, he sat it on the window ledge proclaiming the "King is dead."

The remnant of those standing beneath the window of flames were admonished on the sight of this bloody torment! They were beholding who has the power to do this.... 'Wondering what will the Queen' have to say about this? For all fighting has ceased, in the palace and the castle's grounds out to the moats around the immediate fortress. The servants along with the poor peasants were just looking upon each other bewildered asking, why should we fight amongst ourselves?

There laid 'one-hundred and twenty-souls,' on the castle grounds and inside the palace halls and rooms. It was a 'bloody bath for the Queen's' sake, the whole affair was the doings of the 'Queen,' but there wasn't a living soul who would denounce her...

When the battle of the conqueror's wits had come to an end, and the city's flames had subsided, daytime was shining forthright against the castle's walls.

It was the leadership of one townsman with some authority that proceeded the orders to the crowd it's time to bury the dead.

The restoring of the kingdom's palace and all that remains within he recommended the 'Queen to be reestablished.' In his request he argued the 'Queen had showed' us kindness in our time of need! With her beauty and compassion showed her heart to be delicate and somewhat disturbing. So, I say let us forgive, especially when we need each other for security.

And when her handmaiden had appeared, speaking for the 'Queen' she said, the 'Queen' nodded, I will accept the position of leadership, and I will do the best I can, and I will inform the crowd when direness approaches. They cheered with hopefulness that you will resume your position as the "Queen of Hosts" and take care of all the remnants that stand inside the palace walls. For they voted and there was no – one here that has any objections. This kind Lady got what she wanted again! A master of deception should be her pronoun.

Besides they were all afraid of what this woman could do! Thinking she has the power and magic of a sorcerous, they had the utmost respect for her advice!

The 'Queen assured herself,' naturally they would indulge me, saying who else do we have? In her mind she recalls ten years earlier this encounter with the poor peasants taking over the castle's domain and the King being appointed to that position by all the townspeople, she laughed knowing nothing has really changed, just different faces.

Then the 'Queen stepped out onto the 2nd floor balcony,' and announced with her eloquent voice and her soft- voice the honor and glory that you have shown will be strong for many years to come. For there will be banquets and feasts for many moons and 'I the Queen' accepts the appointment of ruling the castle and all its domain. The 'Queen' stayed in the same appointed position as she had done before, with her adoring beauty and charming splendor, she was back sitting on the "Queen's throne" where all power was given to her once again.

SHORT BREATH OF THE STORY

This story depicts of a ruthless Prince. It's called: *A Prince and his Dark Kingdom*. Now Prince 'Dario' was the ruler and leader in his Kingdom. The year was 1032 A.D. and he ruled as a fierce but rather a deranged man. In his mind he set the rules, and they could change daily. In his deranged contorted mind, his sickness dwelled in the spilling of someone's blood. He would always look for a guilty victim to process through the courts for his legal action of murder.

A Prince and His Dark Kingdom

Being in an isolated fortress of high – stretched wall and controlled by those who have these fanciful clothes they paraded in a straight formal, supposedly with the assumption, a strict fashion of obedience. Far be the illusion of their best intention, for there were still a host of plagiarism participating within the compounds of their joy zone.

But the "prince of leadership Dario" was in fact somewhat content, his disposition commonly dispersed the lucid thoughts of others contending he had the better advice. The prince's deceiving objectives frequently put those who threaten him in a disadvantage position. He thought his cleverness was so crafty even himself would brag on his own deceitful cunningness.

"His Kingdom ventured in the year of 1032 A.D." and was held with the ever- daily changing of "his laws." His philosophical rationing, and his authority as his ruling ever so often; seemed to be unjust to those who witness his depravity. Of course, this has been hampering those for years. He would set up his courts and have the members of his loyal family be the attorneys for the accused, whether for or against. The people in turn would past judgement with their nay or yea decisions.

But they would from the corner of their eyes see the expression on the "face of Dario" before yielding out what the verdict would be! And generally, he would suggest with his arm stretch out to the side of himself and use his thumb to set the verdict in motion, enticing the jurors to rule in favor of his delusional mindset. With his smooth seductive voice and chilling smile, the wheels were turning to get the crowd in a frantic hostile mood, "chanting death – death" to the defendant in question! Depending on the accusation of the accused and his standings of loyalty may decide whether to allow witnesses to favor the person on trial.

If you be one of the naïve who speak out to favor the accused in question, it could lead you to folly to where you find your-selves on trial. Of course, these rulings would suggest what the penalty of the guilty party would be!

If these cases were to reach to the highest courts it was subject to "life or death," and, "if it be death then what form of death," would the accused be subject too? There were no adversaries to challenge him from his dominion. He had the whole land to do what he pleased. His riches were exceedingly beyond the wealth of the people and the land.

His subjects and loyalist depended on his wealth to live a plush lifestyle of luxurious dinners and banquets, clothe in exquisite attire, where they would have dances and music beyond measure.

All these things inside his monastery style castle he had acquired from those less fortunate. His divisive shrewdness was appalling of how he came into possession of the castle and its silver and gold. The apparels of his costumes were subject from musical plays and theaters in which he had stole from those that were living in mire when the economics fell through.

His fortress was surrounded with iron fences and gates the security he had in place were those he chose to keep guard to earn there rationing for the day.

Within the populace of his subjects, he acquired those with talents!

"Dario chose his subjects" from the beggars that would come by to ask for a morsel of bread. The prince would jest to those whimsical sniffles what can you do for me? "For pleasure the prince" picked out, buffoons, musicians, dancers and beauty, to entertain the lively lifestyle of his amusement. Those living in small villages would stand outside his castle crying out for food! His courtiers would approach the prince and inquire; you have visitors at the gate. What do you want to do with them?

"His grinning smugness," would imply be off with them, or 'I'll have their heads!' Shrewdness enveloped within his passion. This delirious onset brought cold feelings inside his head; 'thoughts of murder,' was embarking his conscious. "There will be blood spelt tonight, was forming in his mind!"

Then his dismal state in affairs, subsided for a while, and he gather his thoughts and put them off to the wayward side. He would venture to other rooms of his palace to relax from the irrational foolishness of others.

He would look at the populace of his empire that were living inside the palace, each having their own rooms. And conjure ways to have his subjects accuse each other in malice.

For, he thought it's time for a new trial.

His mind was getting irritated or bored from the jesters in the palace and he started to project different methods to bring them before the courts. He would use his divisiveness to create hostility, one against another.

Then there would be a means for accusations to begin forming amongst their-selves. "Prince Dario" had pleasure watching, the petty arguments that led to guilt to arrive for the "death penalty."

And his legal action of using the courts to justify his thirst for blood to keep others in line brought satisfaction to his desire. And he thought how foolish these peasants are judging their-selves. "For he thought more blood needs to be spilled with the screams of horror!"

This famous ballroom with expensive crystallized chandeliers hanging from a vaulted ceiling and ebony chairs with marble statues would be the parlor to address the courts and bring about social gatherings for expressing any matters that needed attention.

There meetings would be required by rule from "Prince Dario," or there could be punishment for those who didn't show. The room was arrayed with gothic windows of different shades, the first corridor that led the passageway was decorated white as were its tinted windows, the next would be shaded blue, and then came green and the last was decorated with black but the windows were tinted red. "Dario enjoyed the last chamber" it gave him a sense of authority, and blood was its color.

This was the final room where the sentence would be handed out. For illumination there were brazen torches of fire hanging on the walls opposite of the windows. This would give a dazzling-colored accent a scheme of rays that reflected off the tinted glass.

When the accused reached this point of judgement, he knew that the ruling was death! For he had seen this from others before him. His voice would tremble and pled with Dario, and he would fall on his knees imploring him what others have done, begging for their life. This was music to Dario's ear; he would be laughing about how foolish this peasant has been. Then he would agitate the crowd and shout out; "what form of death do we want?"

In his delirious mind he thought there will be "blood flowing on the floor" and that gave him pleasure and a sense of power. His mindset was beyond recognition. He just didn't know what form of death he would enjoy tonight!

He would act as judge and seer, handing down the verdict and announce to the parishioner, "an elected buffoon in Dario's eye's;" the method of execution and his followers would need to vote. This way he thought to himself these foolish peasants will partake in the final decision, was his reasoning. 'His laughter would echo," across the chamber and the populace would laugh with him. They would look at each other nervously with a small laughter, "for fear they could be next!"

The sly gesture that was grafting on his face, thought this will be a "night of torture!" he was witnessing nervous tension amongst the crowd of peasants, which brought "louder laughter from Dario." In his mind these imbeciles were his pawns that he could move on a whim.

"Prince Dario with his boastful voice," would echo out the pleasures that are in stored during the murderess execution. "His raving delirium was thinking what form of death would be pleasing?"

He would mention the music, the dancing and the fatted pigs that will be roasted during the festival. We will bring out the costumes and the theme of this magnificent celebration will be, who will "consume the fatted special!"

"For my punishment of torture will be the roasting of the accused!" We will cook him over an open fire rotisserie and serve him with an apple in his mouth! And we will all 'devour his flesh and the blood will be sprinkled' around the stones of the pit. This will be meat for the poor peasants to eat, so they may fill their bellies, 'while chuckles of amusement,' was showing his heartless expression. The 'laughter coming out of Dario's mouth was bouncing across the halls into chambers with delirious illusions.'

He noticed the "horrifying looks on their faces" of the populace and laughed even louder! The peasants were trying to laugh with him, but the shock of his demise tormented their souls. You could see this through the windows of their eye's, 'the madness of his joy!'

Even the courtiers by his side were in fear by the voracious appetite that he had announced. They thought who dare try to seize the prince with his 'mutilated murder!' They tried pleading with the prince but to no avail. His sick mind was made up. He needed 'blood to ease his soul. '"He shouted to his jesters to stoke the fire to a higher gleam." The winnowing breath from others was useless, he shrilled out in a gaily voice, bring out the sacrifice and have your spindles ready!

The grand course for this evening had arms and legs roasting on an empty pit with "cries of gaiety hollering in gruesome terror!"

Who be you that could take pleasure of excitement, the throbbing of hearts, the anguish hatred of darkness as you watch the "screaming of torture!"

"You ask, is this madness in its first stage of horror?"

The terrifying peasants were witnessing the "freshness of flesh as it was sizzling on the flame!" The 'sharpness of agony had subsided' and the "voice of shrills has vanished" when 'Prince Dario asked,' one of his courtiers for the keenness, slipperiest edge on hand! He took the edge and sliced the throat from ear to ear, "spilling the blood in a pan."

He ordered one of his jilted peasants to bring a pot and have the cook make some savory sauce out of this. Then with what he had in the pan, his grinning gesture, commanded one of his clowns, sprinkle it upon the stones, and suggested he would jest and make merry, or we may require his head next!

When the music and the voices had ceased from witnessing the pleasures of the prince, from "his gruesome madness to his bloody murderous cravings," the peasants were awaiting as if they needed a motion from the prince to make merry again! The masses of the peasants would be standing, looking at each other in dismay, conjuring suspicious false witnesses against their neighbors.

"Wondering who will be the next sacrificial offering." 'Prince Dario' insisted to the crowd this was a celebration to honor the riches of wine, music and merry making. Let us all fill ourselves up to our hearts content. Now begin the music, and let there be dancing, enjoy the festivities for this is a happy occasion that calls for celebration; this will be a day of remembrance that will last all night long.

And the poor peasants in the Kingdom once again went through its monthly rituals of pleasing the desires of the prince.

SHORT BREATH OF THE STORY

The Forgotten Incident is the name of this story: This is about a man whose nerves reflects, back to his guilty conscious mind. It's about an inconceivable act that he needed to do. There was another man who was rather wealthy, and he obtained it from people who happen to fall on bad luck one way or another. In other words, he took advantage of the other family's misfortune. The first man devises a plot to murder the wealthy man for the people's revenge.

THE FORGOTTEN INCIDENT

"Whispers," silent whispers, the stillness of whispers echoing "small sounds.... very.... very small sounds...." voices teetering shallows of "minuet tones.... whispering tones....' small casual tones.... 'Tones uttering.... muttering chilling tones," the constant awareness the flagrant suggestions that keep reminding us of what took place! Visions peering within that are unaccounted for, seem to invite a sense of anxiety to come along, allowing distraught to sink in without warning, asking, what happened? A dismal blindness, a tension unseen, uneasiness that follows, leads you to bring up this "guilty nervousness!"

In your wildest dreams this idea... this careful planning.... this successful accomplishment was dauntless, and fearless, a haughty arrogant cunningness was forming in your voice before you noticed the beginning of a delirious "shake – down!" While shoring up the reassurance of your cleverness, the demeanor of your outward appearance was being threatened! For it's been "three – days passed," since, when the unmentionable task was at hand.

A suspicious confrontation was staring at you when you found yourselves in argument, speaking with hostility before you realized I'm talking to myself! A continuing barrage of attacks would be surfacing, refurbishing the atrocity of your shameless deed. All this has found a way back to initiate the demoralized incident that took place "just three – days back!" "But how.... how could it be...." I kept asking, this was justly deserving, "I kept telling myself."

This sudden agony developed causing you to twitch just thinking about it! But you kept informing yourselves this was a deliberate plan that was set up weeks back.... "Why now.... why!" Must I have a guilty conscious now, when my cold icy veins didn't bother me in the least before the "murderous incident?"

My deceitfulness was ever so casual and calm when proceeding! For I've been watching and plotting in secret of how this event would eliminate the corruptness of the individual, of whom this plan of murder was intended for!

"Oh," I thought at the time how this careful plan could benefit those who got shunned and destroyed from this liar's accusations!

This man possessed countless dishonest allegations that were made-up.... yes, made up.... He arranged things to profit him.... yes...him... Exploitations of those around were dubiously unsettled, for his authority surpassed even the policemen on the streets. Likewise, the judges in the district seemed to be under his thumb along with the mayor.

But I thought nothing is going to stop me from 'my plan......' 'my delirious intentions......' 'an inescapable...... an unavoidable demise' of the so – called bastard at hand! But when the opportunity arose, I tarried, telling myself I wasn't quite ready.... coaxing and encouraging myself there will be other occasions and there are better places to pick for Murder! 'My frightening hesitation' was something I didn't expect, while questioning my own intentions I seemed to pause and wondered, who can we blame!

Looking at the area this insidious manner suggested to me, it would be the wrong time to commit this violent but necessary act. While standing across the street in a shady corner as he entered the cab that had stopped for him, I thought I'll just wait. We were watching intensively his every move and thought he would be gone for a while. A sigh of relief allowed me to breathe normally again. Now was the chance to reconstruct my plan, now was the time to orchestrate how we will carry out and fulfil my expected intentions!

The building he was standing in front of was his private office and his home was on the 2nd floor. As he left while sitting in the back seat of the cab, I decided to cross the street to look and study the surroundings around the entrance to the front of the building. Besides the streetlights just came on and other people were rushing by from a hard day's work, glaring back I went over to glance at the entrance again.

A sagacious grin started to form on my face when I told myself I had found the answer! A shrewd, but quick bloody scene was being portrayed in my mind!

I thought let the lying fat man suffer as he has done to others, his sharp and nasty voice has brought him here in my presence---Let the fat- liar talk and wallow in his own pigsty. Then we began to laugh with an annoying smirk, sounding as if we had already killed him.

His mindful thoughts were remembering the ambiguous nature, that this man would try to perceive as he was tossing families in the street. His riches and greed he would keep them inconspicuous so others wouldn't realize his intent or what his motive was.

This irritable man had the gall to use the commission of land-deeds, ownerships and taxes to waver forfeitures of those who could not pay. Even it was said of the mayor and commissioner the lying maneuvering of laws he used to settle in order to get his way.

He was a cheating, conniving smart - liar that took pleasure in bringing those around to their knees. This has led people to despise this man who thought he was above the law and everybody else. The only people he associated with were those that he could con to provide him the necessary means to add to his portfolio. The remnant of his success required more ownership, regardless of the price, whether man, woman or child. When mentioned to him the horrible causes that he imposed on the less fortunate, his smile.... and...... his laughter would shriek beyond measure the pleasure of his character.

How demeaning.... how shrewd.... how despicable a man could be! This is the profile of the man in question! These are the thoughts I have and certainly others think the same way, but I have made up my mind to do something about it!

Then the dizziness of my mind was struggling within the suggestions that I had made known. My plans were losing sight after a leisurely swoon, which left me in silence. The shadowy memories preceded to come and go. While looking, this event keeps coming back, this hideous device of murder still surfaces!

Very suddenly this plan was coming back to my soul, the sounds.... the motion.... the touch...... the thoughts are reflecting to this justification of Murder! In my weak pondering soul,' I thought I had this worked out! Disparity had somehow entered my thoughts, which took me off course. The tumultuous motion of my heart was loud enough for my ears to hear from the echoes of my frame. The hatred was beginning to build itself and forget the idling swoon from whence it began. A rushing turbulence entered my consciousness, this was the moment that we had to try again.

But the man in question was no – where to be found; somehow, he knew what I was planning.

With a rushing torrent of radical pulsations my blood was swelling, there was nothing to do but wait. I dreaded the stillness of waiting, it felt as though I was being impeded for a purpose. What could the reason be--- now the very beads on my forehead were dripping; this agony of suspense grew intolerable, I had to walk around to get my focus back--- but where---- "where could we go and not miss him again!"

While pacing back and forth a shuddering thought occurred, what if he doesn't come back. A quandaries imposition had put me in an unstable condition while gazing at the stoop of the building. I could feel the edge I once had is starting to diminish with every minute that passes; I tell myself this needs to stop, my horrid plans are to keep my word and do away with him. This endless anxiety keeps haunting me and I need a reminder of who he is!

Twitching in various positions a sudden shock gave way, when the headlights of a cab came up to me.... asking do you need a ride.! Startled by the voice took me beyond my own circumstances. I waved my hand to go on gesturing leave me alone; but this sudden diversion kept me losing my mind again. Watching the shadows bouncing while engaging the lights that struck the mason walls led me to think, is this a dream I'm walking in?

Exasperation settled in my mind and nervousness exalted itself taunting my every move. When will this liar show up! Anger was preceding within as I was standing in an alley on the corner of a building adjacent from where he lived. My weapon was conceived secretly inside the jacket I was wearing for the evening had cooled down. The only lights that lit – up were those on the streetlamps and the little shops that were still open.

This I thought was the first day of my intentions… my actions… my cautious cleverly plan – that I had devised. Will my plot work out as planned, delaying my strategy with all this waiting; ambiguous thoughts of maybe re-calculating the murderous deed, now seems to be in question! Sitting at the corner of the building I found myself furiously rubbing my hair and face, thinking, just stick with the plan!

A perish of animosity perked itself into play, while visualizing the extremity of what my mind has set forth. This shall be a delightful expenditure! This tarrying was gleaming a slyly grin, and my mind for the first time was enjoying the lucid rationality I had in my head.

A profound contemplation came forward, a distinguished aspiration inquisitively set a dramatic picture allowing the thoughts to circumvent while the mind was in another stage of fright. Now the collusive matter stands; this conspiracy of what transpired may need to be explainable. What should the alibi of my actions be, when the deed has been done? I never thought that far ahead! Oh my! This unforeseeable demise has somehow put a glitch in my plans!

I thought simply tell them, 'When it requires me to do so,' I was in another place. Besides when I looked at the analogy, the average sequential sequence will adhere to a culprit; that should lead them to be someone from out of town. At least this was the best lie I could come too. In my divisive dialog this was the only answer I could come up with.

While glooming in a far distance, I noticed a knowingly darkness has loomed; pondering when will he show up…? Then suddenly a cab roared to a screeching halt! The lying fat man finally showed himself when he oft through the cab door. While strolling to his front doors and whistling a tune that made him prosperous with a jolly laughter, he relinquished his key to the entry way.

My adrenaline was increasing, my heart thumping at a faster pace, I thought this is the time. I moved my hand inside of my jacket and felt the handle I would use to proceed the dastardly deed with. A fumbling of my feet had missed the step at the curb, as I slowly walked to cross the street. But this didn't bother me for I had one thing in mind; do want I intended to. Keep with the plan I intended while crossing the street. My focus was getting the fat bastard while I had the nerve to do so!

A frosty cool breeze happened to strike my face as I approached the stoop and standing in front of me was the entrance. A strong sturdy wood ingress was between me and the intention of my infuriated desire! A tapping on the exterior hardwood, I imagined, "I'll play...." a discerning neighbor with a question or two. We will assert a series of concerns within the neighborhood with questions! My first discernment will ask, how you would respond "saying the people on the street have an issue with the increases of taxes," for I knew I could get his attention when it became to a point of money. My thoughts: he must invite me in!

When the door ajar and the man answered, "who be it," I hesitated for a second and then I inquired I'm here for a survey.

His voice in an arbitrary stature asked, what survey, I heard of no survey, 'who be you?'

I'm a concerned citizen and a fellow member of the neighborhood was my response. He jousted with laughter and asked what questions do you have? I preceded calmly with a seriousness of illumination on my face and said it pertains to money sir! This aching tension within my mind, started thinking maybe I should force my way through to eliminate the fat- bastard in hand.... But before I could evaluate this a little further, he fully opened the door and said come on in, so I might know who I'm dealing with!

A chilling smile dashed across his face and in one hand he had a glass of whiskey as he commented, "What's this I hear about money? For I knew he was drinking whiskey because he filled his glass again with a half-emptied bottle on the bar counter.

A fluttering grimace was in his eyes, when he looked toward me, haven't I seen you before? I peered at him saying we might had run into each other at one point of time. Then that chilling despicable laughter when he grunted trying to catch his breath, while chewing on that big stogey he had in his mouth, was deplorable. At that moment it put a gleaning glimmer in my eyes I was ready to pull the handle out of my jacket, then suddenly he turned his back on me and asked, what the question was while filling his glass again…. I flinch as I was shaking my head, trying to snap out of this murderous content…. My mind glanced down……'oh yes'…. there is…. 'mm'………concern that…. property taxes will be on the rise this coming year.

'He laughed and laughed….' He said who put that idea in your head…. Then his laughter commenced in getting louder… it looked as if he heard a good joke; he was so amused that he could barely stand on his feet…

While continually glancing around his office room he had his wet- bar with a refrigerator and a lounge in a small corner of the space. He invited me to come here, and we'll have a drink together, since you've managed to make me laugh.

When I sat on a stool at his wet- bar his breath and slobbering gestures were getting annoying, but he kept rumbling on non- stop… as he looked at the clock on the wall the arms were stretched out to eleven – thirty.…... and he mentioned it was starting to get late. With a glass still in my hands pretending I was drinking and paying much attention with his jabbering relinquishing innuendoes, my mind seems to wander off.

A disgusted and capricious emotion flared, while listening to this arrogant boisterous fat man gesturing the imbeciles that he was dealing with. His laughter was ludicrous and haughty, bellowing languishes and foolishness; a distraught of actions from others was just downright laughable. His erratic composure displayed a mad – man in disguise.

Looking attentively at the situation my mind became perplexed "who was the mad – man here.…... me or him!" His jolly laughter became louder as he was aware of what I was thinking.

I was starting to tremble, my mental stability appeared to exert a painful exertion. I had to get up and walk about to remain calm, or his voice of agitation and demoralizing tautness would win. That chilling spidery slivery of laughter was humiliating me to the point of putting my hand on the wooden handle of my relief of pain!

Ever so gently I grabbed that wooden handle and suddenly thrust that scythe blade quickly puncturing the quant rant of his side; his sudden squeamish voice uttered.... 'What was that for....' As his voice shrilled, I lounged with a second pierce to quiet his soul...... his mouth spewing salvia dripping down his chin as his eyes bulged out with spuriousness, then he proceeded slowly sinking to the floor of his office room.

Finally, silence... complete silence....as quietness.... absolute quietness......proceeded in this house of shame! This bloody task has been done! As if I won a medal. I wipe the blade cleaned and turned all the lights off, my mind thought now the tension is gone as I egressed from the presence of this laughing torment....!

SHORT BREATH OF THE STORY

The fourth story in said book is called: *Sudden Chillness*. In this story it describes about a man that gets a visit by a haunting demon like spirit. This demon is trying to hold him into the pits of hell. He uses all the devices he could to hold the man, but there is a word confrontation. After the battle the Devil himself told the demon that he could not hold anyone who is still in the flesh. After words were exchanged between the three in the fiery pit, the man was sent back to where he was found, before this incident.

Sudden Chillness

The evening of a slithering chillness, the abruptness of aquatints has disappeared, leaving without warning an unsuspected gleam promenading a stirring awe. But when I looked at this carefully a stunning coldness came across, while my eyes were adhering to the providence from whence it began. The etching of lines resembled something that once was there and now it's gone! With a closer look the demeanor I seen had vanished; but as I look even closer the outward appearance was still there!

An outline of a figure was standing upright, laughing with haughtiness; at the languish of my thoughts! This laughter, this smile, grimacing a smugness had you glancing at it twice. With a jilted response I pondered at it in dismay; my eyes were fixated on the image in question. Looking deeply within this recoil of a diminishing black outline with grayish intrusions was protruding the little understanding that I had; it was continually hovering within the area I was standing in. My mind was conveyed where suspicion was causing doubtfulness to circumvent. A vague awareness was announcing and introducing their intentions. This proposed desire happened to look at my conscious. As it was trying to diminish the thought that I had, it consistently began to frame itself into my head.

How I felt so out of touch, as time spiraled along. A casual slight gingerly tension sprung to one side, and I observed; I believe I observed; I noticed a sense of quietness; I believe I notice the frailness of attempted humbleness just beginning; happening to surface, from a wavering contorted face.

Then suddenly the quivering lines drew out of the facile, as uneasiness, a congenial sympathy of one's circumstance, was brought forth not understanding what just transpired.

Then I wondered, who was kidding who, the emotions I felt was contempt and enticing, kept swirling its teasing, laughing at you with no relief! This jittering movement of persuasion looked at me with sneers formulating a gruesome smile; I was hypnotized; my eyes were subjected to the chilling glare of a laughing, continuous smirk. Then my mind seemed to be subjected into a transformative, unknown.

It was as if a reaction of an apostate was looking at me smiling and laughing like a clown. Who, be you I said, standing with a smiley grin! His laughter went into a higher pitch!

His demeanor squalled into louder laughter. As I stood in front of an image that kept laughing at me!

His appearance was somewhat foolish, he was wearing a clown's outfit; hat and clothes resembled a clown even his red-rounded nose looked disturbing.

A jaunty fellow dancing, sprinting; shooting his legs out as if he was humming with an Irish folklore song, but that laughter constantly bellowing the arrogant supercilious giggle from his mouth was intimating.

He flaunted himself from a short distance just for a minute; when I had to look away just for a moment; I noticed he was gone! Then my eyes glanced around in the place from whence I was at, the vision came back to its normal stature. As if I dreamed this all up – my mind – my eyes started to focus harder! I know I didn't dream this all up! I know what I seen! I know what I heard! Where is this weird phantom of a mis- colored dress of a clown be? His outfit with pink, yellow and tangere spots, portrayed in a white pajama suit background with bluish buttons; his red hair sticking out like straw, wedged into an odd stricken black hat, with a purple flower pointing up off a green stem; it appeared his elastic face with whiteness was appalling, dauntless, a harbor of fright seemed to pierce through that tenacious grinning smile of whiteness that supposedly anointed his painted face - ; with red teardrops flowing from his eyes – as it extended to his jaws; floppy feet jumping towards the mid- section of his waist- line; where is he?

This appearance of an elusive clown, where is it; is it "just in my mind?" A disparity had shown its face; conjuring an illusion that was presented inside my head! A streak of a dull dark and soundless day was passing by. A disillusion was coming forth! Where was this oppressive imagination coming from! I know not how it was – but where is it coming from? The glimpse of its initial form was disturbing enough. This insufferable sentiment was eluding the allusion that was in front of me. A dismal portrait was painted even into the sedges of its domicile.

Who be that! How could we withstand the prominence of its success? A staggering prescience was presenting itself. A conscious of an unknown seemed to announce itself.

Will my mind ever relax itself from this unannounced vision from what I saw earlier?

As my head was roaming back and forth, with my eyes peering from side to side, I was waiting for this vision to come back. This obtrusive elusion was gone!

I pierced at this vision but was distracted there was nothing there but stringy lines of mist hanging; swinging in this wavy contorted surrounding I was gazing at.

This dark space was glaring at me wondering if I had a solution. An imaginary outline was portraying, asking who, are you staring at! My mind, my very being was distorted, what am I looking at!

There was nothing there but a dark shoddily space! My illusion was, did I see something strange?

Was there a fragment of my mind going in a direction that I didn't understand? A succumbing of my mind was still hiding itself inside of my head; I pondered again and asked where is this going? A black secret exposed itself saying wake up and we'll show you.

This yielding opened an experience, following a dark gloom that supposedly happened in front of your eyes. A consequential inference was flickering while beginning to form itself! Without notice the abruptness of noises started to happen so suddenly, then suddenly the vision was gone. As we looked around there was silence once again! The shock that dispersed from my imagination struck another confinement. This restriction caused me to doubt myself.

Searching in several different directions I couldn't find where the noise was coming from. A faint, but noticeable query sound jeering a slight whispering giggle was protruding through a foggy glare. I thought I seen a smile; while I heard laughter, tormenting the area from where I was standing in.

Then suddenly I seen a jiggle of movement moving quickly inside the grayish air, from whench I was gazing at; --- what looked like vagarious outlines dancing following the midst of its shadowy blend. A dimness of conforming lightly images was protruding lines of streaky rays and it had projected itself in the darken atmosphere. This wavering apostate was there and now it's gone!

What was this I asked? I even looked at it again and inquired once again, who is there?

This shiny spectrum was announcing itself! A glimmer of sparkle gazed at the darken blackness and then suddenly it was gone! It vanished, disappeared into nothing; now the blackness stared at me with no reflection. As I pondered with dismay, I questioned it again, what do you want with me and who are you?

The quietness, the chilling stillness, stood all alone floating in the slumbering air while the misty whiteness was wiggling as it was evaporating into the upper region of its whispering domain. I was surprised and shocked of what I saw!

This unannounced suspicion seemed as though it was playing on my mind. A daunting intimating quaver was the sense my nerves was unfolding. A vigilant alertness was behind these bulging eyes, as my limbs started trembling from this unknown vaporous substance or was it a vision from another sphere!

But I kept asking where is this intermittent luminous reaction coming from? A twinging phosphor glow had enacted a sizzling silent, humming, and this shiny slippery sizzle seem to dance in the darken night as if the jagged edges seem to disappear when it reached its end.

Then this vestige would repeat itself; a brief flash crackled and suddenly it disappeared once again.

My eyes just jumped when this repeated abruptness sprang out of the darkness that I had glanced at. It reminded me as though electricity was climbing a pair of solid conductors and when it reached the end of the line it jumped and whipped its cackling tail into thin air. Then the vision was gone! This force of hued brightness would jump so quickly looking for something to cling too.

I stood there amazed or was it shock, my feet I noticed couldn't move. It seemed to come closer as I pondered, wondering what, what was it going to do! This darken atmosphere was coming closer; surrounding me as if it was going to engulf me like I was part of a shadowy dispersion that was in its way. As this glary light came towards me; it surprisingly went right through me. I could feel the impulse of its tension protruding past the skin I was wearing. My being was traumatized, and an unknown disturbance had encircled the area I was standing in.

Then laughter started bellowing from a form of a gruesome chilly smile and a vision of the clown was back. His humorous giggle was taunting me, an allusive grin he put forth on his face, as if his expression of jeering was mocking me!

This cold sneer enticed me and suddenly an opening of his mouth laughed even louder as his sharpen canine hostility grew deeper into the reproach of his stance. Then the violent tempest of air flew past the area I was standing in; and when the winds had calmed down and subsided, the image I saw was gone.

My mind, my very being has become; chilled to the bone of this imaginary clown, or was it imaginary, now it seems as if I'm going delirious, or could it be a substitute from an extreme mental excitement, but I kept asking myself what; what does he want with me! I could feel my nerves twitch and my eyes were bugged out leaning towards the direction from whence this has all started.

Once again there was silence in this gloom of night; looking at the place where there was no movement.

A quiver of nervousness had my eyes twitching, while my suspicious mind kept roaming about, as if it was trying to inquire; frowning; a notion of a suspended guise; a strange deceiving appearance; or was this just a false pretense that my mind had somewhat conjured up, as it was looking; this delusional unknown had inconspicuously led my mind to a scene that wasn't there!

Then a tremor of doubtfulness took over, while my thoughts began looking into the distance darkness. Blackness started rolling and forming all around covering even the clothes I was wearing.

Then shades of grayish shadows were floating sporadically in the air; dancing while roaming gently along the foggy sky, as the mist in its perpetual motion swaggers from here to there.

This gloominess was silent, but the sounds I heard within my head were screams; cries shouting out, "help us, help us,"; "out of this torment" this silent torment is bringing about me inwards, towards madness. In my mind, I could hear pain from the shrills flashing by as they were casually crossing the sky. An eerie feeling of ghastly eyes being taken away as they just floated by to another realm. These anguish, terrifying looks of terror from their faces and shrieks of horror from their contorted mouths; bellowing moans of shrills. I glared at this vision wondering if it was real!

The groans from petrified faces with their mouths opened looking so dreadful as this unsettling appearance kept gliding along the vaporizing mist. I could see their blurry eyes shouting out in pain. While the slow movement of wind consistently took the faces of these foggy outlines moving them to another dark space and when they had left; there was more behind them. I was spooked from following those faces from one dimension to another.

It seemed like myriads of ghostly images swaying, twisting, or wrenching out of its usual form into one that is grotesque; a chilling whiteness; a dimness flowing with deformative outlines as you observed the grimly frown found on those faces. The shuddering of their mouths constantly moaning as the tension of fear were in their eyes. Screams echoing against the inner walls while following the allusive streams that they seemed to be suspended from. Frightening lowly shrills I kept hearing when the clown came back, and the picture of the misty faces floating into the foggy air were gone! Once again, the darkness came back to re- align the view in hand.

Low key screeches I could hear, or were they screeches, this slurry sound was bouncing so gently along the congested confusion of slightly condensed vapor.

These repeated echo sound waves were starting to get unbearable; loud enough to notice, but quiet enough to antagonize your nerves. How has this timid irritating noise reaching the place that intimidates my mind into a torture hull? As I stood their taking the agitation of disturbing seditious noises, I kept asking myself why, why is there a horrid of sullen sadness quaking over me.

Then the clown showed himself, he began to laugh; then he chimed in, don't you know the destination that you fell in! His brazen voice startled me when he said that. My eyes were fixated at him when his shameless laughter got even louder.

This ludicrous contempt that appeared in his scornful eyes seemed to bring a sense of flaring embers sizzling in the pit of fire! A damnation of faces started once again roaming across the open slurry sky. The anguish depiction of their faces looked as if they were constricted from the vision I had seen earlier. Their voices were uttering in an unformal dismay! A hollering of unconventional spuriousness appeared; dis-ingénue as the uncontrollable shrills kept insinuating the hidden darkness, that an abyss of the unknown was real.

A slyly jester from the clown corresponded and asked do you think this is real? His slivery sliding tongue laughed and jolted where do you think you're going? I was disjoined from his interaction, I glared away with discontent. His vigorous voice seemed to get louder. Do not look away for I'm talking to you! My sense told me to stay away. This disruption of a silly clown needs to go away.

He told me I'll send you to journeys that will bring you back to your senses. I noticed there was going to be an interaction and it was going to take place soon! My mind was made up the sooner the better!

A transferring of my being, my spirit was sent to visit a treacherous cavern of dark souls as I whistled along with the haughty gloom of inconspicuous white outlines to a place of doom. When I rescinded to the place of the unknown, I seen they were dazed and obscured; eyes peering at me. These contemptuous cold eyes from those that were being tortured from their past lives were being introduced to me; from a clown with despicable, slumbering yellowish eyes.

His voice announced the reasons why they were here. These poor victims in chains wondered around with continual torment from the devils of their masters.

A chilling torment of those caught in the web, a continual torture of the demons overseeing the punishment of those who got stuck in this house of horror. This damnation inside the house of an infernal crypt had me astounded. And the gatekeeper just smiled and laughed in his make – believe clown outfit- and said, were counting on you to be next.

After hearing his sagacious foresight, I lean back to get away from his deplorable acquisition. It was a standoff of his challenge versus mine!

This demoralizing hindrance that he oversaw, thought that he had the upper edge! But I stood there with glazed eyes fixated on his treacherous smile and blurred out, I'm not willing to come. His laughter just echoed across the hollow chamber. Then he reminded me you don't have a choice! I peered at that cold grinning laughter and thought I'll just chuckle back.

When he observed the knowledge and stubbornness I had known, he started walking around with tones of contention within his eyes. Mumbling in a quaint but noticeable disposition he started thwarting, no flesh is going to get the better of me.

I could see and he could see that he would have to come up with a better plan. While conforming with another suggestion, deceitfulness entered his train of thoughts! At that point as he was walking behind interiors within the darken abyss, I seen he was hiding his appearance of what I seen earlier.

Then suddenly a draconian appearance appeared with a slithering wingspan of ten – feet width appeared, while his head and face showed profusions of reddish texture as the ivory curved horned spikes were projected from the top of his head.

A shriek of iniquity was shouting beyond the everlasting bellowing sounds of heinous atrocities. How dare you shun me in my own presence. He kept reminding me I was his; there was nothing I could do to escape from his commands. His towering appearance looked down at me, his un -relinquishing demands was overpowering me, trying to make me surrender my objective -, my purpose -, my own liveliness -, he tried to make it appalling even into my own eyes. This confrontation that I find myself in, had me gathering my wits, of how did this all come about?

My conscientious thoughts were pondering within; when I decisively started examining what was right and what was wrong! It seemed to me as if I was taken for granted. Who was this deterring demon, what does he think he is? Trying to instill fear, anxiety, and trying to cause doubt to circumvent my very thoughts. I say who is he!

As I observed the shrewdness of his authority, his shearing voice was trying to break me into something deplorable. A resentful evil was coaxing me to admit I was abhorring.

This consistent discouragement of my nature being detestable, a living disgust was playing on my emotions trying to make myself to admit I was horrible; an incurable demise of my worthiness was nothing better than death and torture.

A feverish animosity became evident that the devilish lies were announcing the game plan of what they had in hand.

Anything they could use to rebuke me, conjuring erroneous acts; fallowing guilts of beguilement, fore- as; the wiles of their hatred are deep. I heard cries from those around while their masters were continually punishing them into a screaming oblivion.

Those horrid shrieks were gasping for ease, as those distributing the inflections were just laughing with content. How demeaning the exposure of contemptible hate has brought forth justice. I found the heat in this closed abounded Abaddon scouring with excruciating fire and steam. My breath was panting for more air. The shrilling voice of laughter had once again echoed the words, who's your master!

A discerning thought approached within my mind, questioning the abrasiveness of a quandary quarrel that somehow had us face to face. This uncertainty put him on the defensive side of the discussion. While my mind had relaxed for a moment, just for a second or two, suddenly I realized that I had made a mistake. He came back to announce that I was here to stay! A vicious maneuver on his part had me suspended, somehow, I lost my concentration of what I should have said next.

Then his harsh laughter bounced off the corners of stones, echoing pierces of sharpness throughout the darken cavern I was stuck in; the eyes of witnesses with their drab appearances were shaking their heads. Even the tormentors were grinning with their snide smiles; a chilling anticipation was brought forth wondering when will the gatekeeper drag me in. I gazed back; - told him not so quickly! There are other negotiations to consider.

Who are you that decides my fate? Haven't you sweep me up without letting me make my own choice? Who gives you the power and authority to bring me here? With a strong fiery voice, I pronounced with sternness, I refuse to accept your invitation. As my eyes glared with hostility, he looked at me with amusement.

While I stood and watched him, his posturing laughter had somewhat diminished, he stood still there, with an angrily grim on his face.

The faces of those around were stunned, I could suddenly see their eyes glaring at me in dis-belief. Now as he roamed about in the inner lairs of darkness, he came back out in his clown outfit. His cunning conniving voice whispered you're here with us to stay.

There has been no one who denied me or questioned my command or even denounce my authority. "Who do you think you are," he answered back. He went on to boast; how will you leave from this house of inequity?

For there are no counsels to adhere for advice, there are no courts to submit your argument with, and there is no-one here to plead your case, so, I say again, how will you leave from this place, for there is no other place you can go, you have nothing to bargain with. The craftiness of his under- lying depravity put me in a corner. As I studied his threaten demeanor, I tarried to find the answer that would be suitable.

This exchange of cleverness; a deceptive means of putting one off balance has worked well with him. His hyperbolic voice showed an excessive display of tricking you into something that you didn't expect. I kept thinking what my response should be! This laughable clown was enjoying himself, keeping me confused as his words kept repeating the iniquities of what he had said earlier.

A flaunted expression crossed his face, a crit'tur smile formed across his lips; a tenacious grin seemed to stretch from his mouth to extend to his ears. In this fiery of heated burnt-out stench, his laughter became louder; and he announced who has the better advantage. And as he stood there with ridicule written all over his face, his laughter became even louder. Those that witnessed the outcoming of his boldness became construed to the possibility of his content. A venture of his nobility was at hand. He knew the objection was critical; fore he had known; the time spent in his acquired dominion would not be wasted.

For there was no way he would let those below know he was fallible. There was only one thing that stood in his way of being infallible, in that he knew; was the one who had a shinnery light then he did. A remembrance came to forewarn of what happen from days back. A discovery of what transpired from days years; was the consultation that stuck in his head.

A vigorous voice illuminated with a thunderous shout; in which he had the cavern and caves shaken to disrupt the actions being displayed. A demon even higher than his stance. The devil himself asked the accuser what have you brought into this house of shame? For his face lured with a quicken constraint, when the chief darkness came to complain. The feature of his character shown something of a chimera. A fire breathing monster with a ram's head, a lion's body being displayed with a tail that represented a serpent's trail. Who is this as it tried, to enter into my thoughts! A ferruginous beast of iron and heavy-laden metal happened to be in front of us! And it seems he was the successor in this flare of flames.

I questioned this accusation that stood in front of me? His quench and underlining grin gave a quivering smile. His stature never even gave a response! His dominion was above my stance. A chilling but known formic was starting to perceive from his lips! And when my mouth opened to question this hoax, his demeanor spoke of a place not yet known! He silenced me on a whim, for I didn't have a chance to get my question out!

He furiously looked at the gatekeeper and asked what's the problem? Can you not simply bring in a heart of stone? For this human is mortal, and not ready for everlasting punishment.

The anger from his gruesome face announced the hostility that could take place. A tremor started to form in my mind, when suddenly he directed his attention my way. He informed the demon, what made you bring a mortal to this place? While he was explaining to his master, a dauntless suggestion was put forth in my head! I asked dubiously! Sir, you flattered us; you didn't tell us of the solemnities of eternity; for you spoke to us feebly and faintly.

Who will dare dwell upon the awful wrath of God? Who gave you permission to take my soul to bear into fire and hear the torment of hell for all eternity? For my redeemer has given me life! I stared at him, and he noticed the light shining forth upon my face and quickly told the demon send him back to where you found him.

The glowing image that I portrayed from my name was faithful and true. And I shouted this is "my Jesus." A quivering frown was pronouncing the agitation that lied upon his face.

Before I could blink my eyes, I was standing in the darken evening looking at the slithering chillness, from whench I started. A prominent wind had gushed away, and silence was once again in this place.

Short Breath of the Story

This man is caught in the darkness alongside a wall with a tan suited man at the end of a lane. The shadow who stays with the darkness tries to hide itself when a gleam of light, ever so often pierces through the clouds above. This man happens to see the tan suited man get stabbed at the end of the lane and he eventually died. This story depicts a familiar likeness to himself. This story is called *A Dark Moment*.

A DARK MOMENT

The darkness was shown, as it exhorted itself while listening to the shadow that followed, when a glimmer of lightly dim spectrums was announcing their whereabout. This gleaming activity caught the attention of the shadow was dreading. The darkness stood there wondering which direction, is this going to send me. It pondered, "as I stood there watching," this filtration of a slow-moving glow heading for the corners of where the darkness lied. While gazing at the white- lighted wave lengths approaching; "I see the grayish-shadow trapped in a triangle;" my thoughts focused on where this darkness is running too. As the darkness started to disappear, hiding, I could hear a form of crying; fearing the screams of flames that were touching its surroundings. Sounding as fire off a burning coal, yelling out shouts of pain!

Standing alongside a wall where the light had finally shown up to relinquish its brightness, I stood there waiting. Glaring away from the enlighten barrier, a fragment happened to lay on the ground from a distance. In this once darken unlighted alley there laid a figure of a body at the end of the lane. Upon staring, it appeared there was a tan suited trench coat the man was wearing; but in this hostile environment I didn't want to know. A stranger ran from the scene with a bloody stiletto in his hand, as his head and face were hidden behind the brim of his hat. It just happened; he got a glimpse of where I was at. But he kept going in his own stylish way as he suddenly turned the corner.

There were moans creeping along the pavement of where I was standing, the lightly sheer voice echoed "TRAITOR!" My consciousness was in distraught; telling myself I need to stay away. But the slight murmur was consistent, constantly bellowing the sound "TRAITOR!" I decided to turn and glance at the figure of a tan overcoat as the man inside kept pressing on the words I heard earlier. His blood was spilling on the cement, his face laminated against the alley roadway.

The mumbling contorted noise went from a voice to a slur; and suddenly the lonely silence prevailed. The violence subsided for a moment, the bluish- blacken clouds started to cover the area above, and once again the darkness came back to relinquish its domain.

This sudden black- out approached very quickly after the demise of the so- called tan suited man had exhausted his last breath. Now it was rather enticing; perhaps even dauntless of what may come next. This horrid quietness, the chilling disarray had me looking in both directions; a suspicious gloom seemed to be focusing its drab appearance my way! As I slightly moved my head from one side to the other, my eyes were piercing through the pandemonium it felt it was in.

This place of disorder had me baffled. Confusion set – in and I was asking the heat of the air where in the blaze's am I in? The pounding of thumps was coming from an echo as it extended and reached the end of the lane, where I was standing. This soft-spoken muddling voice uttered you're here with us to stay- -. Upon hearing this whisper only once, did I hear it, a sense of dread-ness, a fear of horror started to enter my thoughts.

This allusive sound had me in suspense dramatizing where is here, so I asked again, 'where is here?' Nothing but darkness formed around me! The touch of its shadowy dimness made me shake and quiver; a feeling of a presence was here, but I could not see it! My mind began to quake from darkness that I didn't understand. My imagination was going beyond what I've seen or heard! I found myself beginning to talk within, perhaps mumbling, then I started thinking what have I become?

The drowning of noises was beginning to run alongside the blackness, and the walls were peering its laughter, through the dreariness that engaged, during its splendor delight.

A frightening exposure was glaring in the direction of blackness of where this had all started. Witnessing the terror that began in

56

the darkness at the end of a lane had me in a stressful convulsion. A sicken and distracted feeling started forming in my abdomen, it found a way to climb slowly and enter the secrets of my mind.

A voice, an utterly quiet sound was speaking to my conscious saying, runaway – runaway-- go home --; But when I looked around there was nothing but darkness ---! I asked, where shall I run -- tell me where -- it's too dark, there's no place to go ---; I would be lost; then I thought am I not lost now?

This was the moment I pondered --- did I hear a gentile hush of laughter--Am I for sure I hear laughter ---? This leisurely smirk was taunting my quietness --It seems I'm stuck in this dreaded alley of a lane in darkness.

While my eyes were sliding back and forth from side to side within my eye-sockets; watching every detail that sprang forth I heard the darkness was laughing --- then I presumably wondered what detail -- this is stillness beyond any; even over- ceding the breath I was taken. A chilling numbness was protruding through the very things I was thinking! Looking back at the figure I had seen earlier the darkness covered the pavement I was seeking. Then the shock became me; I doubted the selection I was glancing at! While questioning my memory, I was assured it was to the left; but after the darkness subsided, I was standing in the wrong position.

Paranoia settled in and brought forth a distraction; my conscious was gazing at a wall that was empty with greyish – dullness, and it started to puncture the illusion I was in --- I called out for the blackness and it did not adhere! The masonry was subjected to the glimmer of a once glittered wall. I asked the darkness that surrounded me where's the figure of the tan- suited man?

A nudge, a push or perhaps a suggested insinuation had directed me to glare; very carefully to the right from where I was standing. This mysterious mist floating through the alley prevented me from determining if there was an image that once laid, on the cement floor, at the end of the lane. A fiery haze of luminous heat had vehemently slid by, singeing, the outer edges of the darkness. I heard mutters of displeasure groaning, as the darkness began to run along, towards the quivering corner ----. Who be this that hides itself in the blackness!

Nervousness had set- in, once again were looking, to and fro; but the blackness was too dark to see. Tension began culminating, reaching past its breaking point. Clamorous bells were ringing inside my head. These vociferous sounds were echoing along the out- stretched wall. My mind was focused on these noises that were re-surfacing in which we heard -- at least we believe we heard ---. Earlier from the end of the lane.

And now the slithering glimmer had once again moved, when the over- headed darkness had taken its place. A blindness, a quietness had allowed itself to circumvent along with the darkness, while we found ourselves still standing beside the wall. It was as it seems; the looming obscuring mist had not ended.

A dismal frown was forming; as I seen the shadow starting to casually flow along the darken wall; touching the edges of the wall while traveling its length to the end of the lane; over- sieging the figure still lying on the ground. As it entered the stillness of the tan-suited figure, it disappeared, and I didn't see it again. This slightly murky- mist had vanished and suddenly I seen the tan- suited trench coat, with a brown tinted brim hat lying on the paved roadway.

A disturbing notion ran through my mind, a bloody scene was being portrayed, perhaps a premonition of something strange. I began asking myself where did this shadow go? It's always been with the darkness since the beginning; why would it suddenly hide from the gloominess, the bleakness, of the darken surroundings, that put me here!

A frightening curiosity....; entered by surprise......, it took the darkness as it was screaming...... while I watched it running towards the crevice of a tightly knitted corner. A brief but dimly gleam protruded from the outside for a second....; only for a moment......; then, perhaps another second......; and as it egressed from the darkness, the darkness slowly but cautiously preceded to come back out.

A gentile whisper I heard.... I think I heard.... for the area was completely silent and dark once again. This soft voice urged me to follow the wall to the end of the alley. A calmly discreet voice was so low, so minuet, that I could barely hear anything. It seems very odd and strange that I couldn't see where this quiet sound was coming from! It challenged me; coaxed me; come; walk along the wall. Follow the corridor to the end of the lane.

There were subtle hints, slyly tones, anxious suspicions, as I felt it trying to penetrate me…., to get me…., to look pass my fears. My conscious looked beyond; it dreaded this sound, this creepy, uncanny voice; but ever so slowly I brought my foot and took a step……; just one at a time….; over- seeing the distance of the wall, where the tan- suited figure was lying. Even in the darken air I could see where I needed to go.

Aghast I was, for I was trembling, was the delusive appearance of my mind overcoming the integrity that once was there; I sense; I'm dreading this walk to a place that's not desiring; standing, and having a wall guide me to a frighten darkness; to who knows where!

The response of my limbs and my slow pacing had me shaken; I found the tension; an unannounced quivering of my knees told me to keep going, while I took one foot further. This never ceasing darkness kept pushing….; the shadow from the lying tan- coated victim encouraged me to come closer…...!

Still there were several steps to take as the shadow whispered to me, to come closer…. My eyes were drawn towards the tan- suited overcoat of where the figure was lying. As I approached, so gingerly, so steady with quietness and stillness, I was close enough to bend and ponder; as I glanced at the face of the victim in the tan- colored trench- coat; hench there was enough glimmer of dimly specters that frightened me! The further I looked the more I realized the facial expression on his face was familiar!

I stood over him wavering; this frowning stature of a man with one side facing down; I could see the one eye glancing at a figment of darkness. I stared amazed; disturbance began when the image of the man's face was me…...!

I questioned it; how could this be? How could this be me when I'm standing here…...!

Short Breath of the Story

The sixth story in said book is called: *On the Wall*. This frightening story tells about a man who sees and hears things that no one else does. He keeps contemplating to himself whether he's just nervous or is he going mad. The eerie chilliness that he goes through to try to keep some form of sanity as he hears souls screaming is beyond his capability of his own sanity.

ON THE WALL

Gloominess approached with a shade of cloudiness, a reflection you just happened to see, from a stained- steel mirror. Evidently a window has been opened to welcome an uninvited guest. This frightening movement of darkness seems to follow me, clinging on my every move. A careful watch over my shoulder to confirm if this deadness of a shadowy light has caught up to me, makes me quiver not knowing what to expect! I wonder, who's living behind my eyes!

Somehow it has made known its intention, it has become a daily routine of my life, my thoughts, my illusions, and a decision was made to allow an intruder to enter my mind of a nervous, so–called madman!

"Who me mad, 'no not me', maybe nervous," "but not mad!"

This unbecoming sharpness allowing the minds keenness' to in – heighten our hearing and seeing brought an intense feeling of suspicion; had us looking around corners and doors, fearing somebody was watching. As my mind wandered in different directions, I seen visible sights. We were at the brink of a formidable breakdown! This visible insight allowing us to hear and see through the walls and ceilings that surrounded us was bizarre and uncontrollable.

This strangeness was continuously expressing itself, trying to confirm your mind is relaxed asking yourselves what, what are you worried about! An odd look from this fear had me ponder, at an unknown image! Fright has introduced itself_causing your voice to cry out in silent agony._

An acute observation of what was happening around me calmly allows me to tell you about this story.

"Would I be mad," when we could tell you this story; would the depths of hell stop us from talking. Could this be Madness!

"No just nervous – so – so very nervous!"

When this dark image came along, we had no unfavorable displeasure with him. I do not recall when the first idea entered my mind, but once conceived I couldn't let go!

A madman couldn't tell you about the details like we can.

You should have seen how wisely I proceeded; "I was going to kill it! My mind was made up; "I was going to kill it!" but I thought, "Oh," I should be so 'clever – and cunning' about how we're going to plan this out!

This breach of experimental violations was done in 1905, this adventitious of criminality on patients didn't seem to send a red- flag to anybody. All is well written on one's own behave. I see the fears showing in their eyes, I see the fear of depreciated worthlessness, I see the fear of hopelessness, I suppose those institutions didn't recognize the hapless unconditional of loneliness. Death has become a silent event in this asylum. Fortunately, my mind was in a dismal affair not needing shock treatment, as others have experienced. Some have gone through this process without authority. I smelled poison in the darkness as I heard souls screaming within. Some have seen delusions of not being able to speak coherently again. My mind expands what do they expect?

This strangeness wasn't just about him! Others have felt estranged also. But he seems to look and find strange circumstances. I was intrigued, it wasn't about him following me, nor was it about him looking at me from beyond my shoulders.

He didn't seem to disturb me as we 'walked or stood' about. "Somehow when I was sitting still" 'this feverish anxiety came along side me,' "that was when the time of darkness showed its presence." It was as if he was 'taunting me' that started this whole episode of horror. I see my soul, screaming again.

As the hours and even the minutes went by it began to haunt me, leaving me not alone. I would try to find places to hide so I would not see him again.

When the darkness showed itself was when I shuttered in seclusion.

During the morning hours when we had our breakfast together, he seemed to be a nice fellow and he didn't bother me in the least. Rather we seem to get along extremely well, of course, I didn't see him very much, it was as though he was busy someplace else.

When the lunch tray was brought in, we would sit at the table talking to – one another, reminiscing about the day we had separated from each other. His discernment seemed to be within my suspicious approval. So, I thought!

It didn't even bother me when he led me around, while 'walking or standing 'alongside me.' "Somehow when I was sitting still," he kept moving about, after the darkness showed its presence, it was as if he was 'terrorizing me into submission' that started this whole nightmare thing. I was becoming petrified and delusional! My soul was screaming at the window again!

As time went by, it began to haunt me, leaving me not alone! I would try to persuade myself that this wasn't real.

This insidious occurrence lasted for days, perhaps weeks, not knowing what to expect! My mind was being disrupted by the events that had evolved from just last week. I stood there in awe, wondering or perhaps pondering what I should do next?

As the morning hours went by, this fellow beside me didn't seem to be noticed or even fearful. There were times I would walk along the halls, and this fellow was no place to be found. It was though he was busy doing something else.

As noon approached a lunch tray would be brought in, at this time we would talk sitting at the table. We would stare at each other glaring into the empty room, is there anything else to share during our morning affairs?

'I thought to myself' would a Mad- man been as cunning as I was? When we could hold a conversation with each other. I would be so calm and collective as how I would speak and talk, a steadiness within my words we used was not to have him suspect anything unusual or give him any definition of intrusion or any idea of infringement upon his privacy. Oh my, do I have to watch my language. Does my language make a difference? This appearing translation occurs when talking with audiences.

When evening came and the lights were on, and I had received my medicine to sleep on my cottage bed that this episode would start again. I thought, Oh my God. I'll be starting a new relationship with something or someone I won't recognize or even know about. Fear came back into my eyes, and I couldn't sleep right. As I stared at the ceiling, I found myself getting very weary of the darkness and its chilling coldness. An unusual frame within myself noticed something wasn't quite right. The pitch-black darkness was showing me a different view.

While lying on my bed, the dark skeleton would come through the window." Something I've been witnessing for the last few nights!

I was in a hopeless situation inside this room where I stayed, entry of confusion has my soul screaming again!

As it was moving about on the wall it was dancing upon; above our head." I pondered through the skeleton as it showed itself on the wall. I began noticing his tautness, I could feel him encouraging me as he entered my room. An actual enchantment of doom was the sounds we heard squeaking on the wall! It was coming through the shadowy window of the noisy glass-stained window, with bars on it!

I would hide my head under the pillow on my bed to get away from the screeches we heard coming through the 'shadowy window of death.'

Other nights I was hiding underneath my bed, to get away from the horror of what I seen. This fear has been growing in me for the last few days, and we can hardly stand it anymore. I question myself to help me from myself, then I saw myself screaming about my mental health.

We kept telling ourselves this was just the sound of a scuffle crossing the floor, or merely a cricket making a single chirping sound or perhaps the wind was whistling by with a soft tune.

But nothing could take me away from that 'dark skeleton moving on the wall!' "For the last six – nights' we've been going through the same ordeal, when will it leave us alone?

It was as if it enjoyed itself watching me be tortured by its sounds and movements that led me to the "brink of no return!"

"The chilling agony" 'of my eyes' holding steadfast on the swaying movement with the sound of its noise was getting unbearable. I could hear the dreadful eerie sounds with its piercing cry's getting loud --- and louder --- it became so loud we must scream or die!

I couldn't stand it anymore! I went up to the 'window beside the wall' and started pounding my fists against the wall, in my bloody anger!

The orderly and the nurse on the psych – ward rushed in from the screams, and 'found Frederick Harris dead,' with his hands over his eyes. His hands were covering his blank pale face while he was lying flat on his back.

His 'blood – shot eye's,' were fully opened staring straight ahead, and his mouth looked though it was trying to scream as he laid there in stillness.

His hands were bloody as he was striking the wall of his madness. His hands and knuckles were torn up! It looks like he was 'fighting for his sanity' said the nurse to the orderly.

Julie the nurse asked Thomas, did he ever mention having any problems_or being scared in any way? He responded, by saying, he did seem to keep things to himself. But I did notice he was frightened of something. But he would never tell me! They both stared at the 'blood dripping wall' with bloody smears stretching to the barred window on the wall.!

They did notice the 'shadows' from the old willow tree outside his room moving about 'on the wall.'

A dairy was found under his mattress where his daily entries were written down. In his last entry it read, "Can't stand the movement on the wall.'" I'm going to kill it, before it kills me!" "Kill it, Kill it!"

When the doctors showed up in his room, they couldn't figure out what caused his demise. But they knew he was 'frightened to death.' While the two doctors talked in private, the orderly said to the nurse in a hush way, just watch they have no idea what cause his death, they will make this report as simple as possible.

On his death certificate they stated. "Death by Natural Causes."

SHORT BREATH OF THE STORY

This story is called: *A Stranger in a Saloon.* A cowboy rides into a windy dusty abandon town in the year 1877. After him and his horse rode 40-miles, they were tired and besides the wind was getting unbearable. He puts the horse in the stable as he checks out the town and he settles into a place called Last Stop Saloon. He finds out that this town has been a ghost town for 10-years. He finds an old bottle of an unopened whiskey bottle and after he naps from drinking too much the town comes alive, and he wakes up. This will repeat itself showing different scenarios.

A Stranger In A Saloon

A continuous scattering of invisible winds was blowing, showing a formation of spasms as it went through the sections of a unique dismal portion of a town, they called "Whispering Willows." "Cries and hollering shrill" was bellowing, as the wind went against the structures while it echoed screeches along its edges and wood slats. As this cool breezy announcement was approaching, it sent disturbing notions that it was getting -close to you. While the bells of a nearby church was chiming and whining its own familiarity, it brought an -unknown hearing, sending tingling in your ears which brought confusion from a rustling nameless signal; echoing alarms constantly ringing in your ears; they would remind you, there was an intruder, but you didn't know where it was coming from!

"A stranger on a spotted horse," was noticed while trotting gently inside this windy town, wondering where everybody was at! He could hear the bells but was not disturbed by them. He could feel the wind whistling along his horse and even his neck. This sire with his spotted attire was a horse with prestige. He always kept his head high, unless the sands of wind were blowing too high. Then his head bowed down to keep the sand from entering his eye lids. Even the man on the saddle was wearing a bandana across his face. This dreaded sandstorm was creating a blast beyond any-bodies expectations. Riding slowly through town as the wind and sand was bouncing off him, he realized that his horse as well as himself needed a break and try to wait out this storm of grainy particles that keep dancing on their faces.

Upon entering down the middle of the road, looking side to side at the grassy weedy high grounds, he seen tall withering elm and willow trees straggling in rotted small groups and a sign leaning over saying, "Welcome to Whispering Willows," Population was bleeding its paint into the board, to where you could not read it. As the rider approached this town of abrupt windiness, he looked from building to building to see if there was anybody witnessing his presence within this windy town. He proceeded on his horse, until he seen a sign above the entry saying, "Last Stop Saloon." There was nobody around, even the wind as it blew from one structure to another didn't even notice anybody around. Then suddenly there was an image of a woman standing inside the structure that he thought he would enter.

As the cowboy got off his horse, he realized the white ring around his horse's one eye, and said steady up Shiner, that's what his name was when he first bought him 3-years back.

As the wind became more violent, he stuck Shiner, his horse on the leeward side of a building. And he promised he would try to find water and feed.

If you looked closely at his peculiar eye, he had a silver lining surrounding that one eye, as it shone with stunning--ness and a particular jewel showed off his presence. He was a fabulous horse that no- one could deny. As he strutted with elegance and pranced like a genuine prince, he was noticed even in elegant towns.

While the cowboy dismounted, he looked carefully up and down the street, he seen nothing but a few tumbleweeds blowing from here to there. This deserted town almost coalified as a ghost town.

Upon entering this windy shadowy town, he noticed there was a livery stable just about 200 - feet down the road. As he pondered, thinking to himself we just traveled about 40- miles today and I'm tired. He lightens up the strap when he lifts the stirrup underneath the saddle before they started walking to the stable, so the horse could breathe a little easier. Which made the saddle looser. This gusting wind was bustling hard enough to make it difficult to walk in. When he approached the stable, he made sure all the stalls were open and said to Shiner, the place is yours. Eventually he took the saddle off and the bit and nozzle strap that was stuck around his freedom and told Shiner, I'll check on you later.

Do what you want and let the pieces fly. While the wind was gusting along the center of town, his thoughts focused very carefully on this eerie feeling this town brought upon him. As his mind was swirling, he thought something wasn't quite right. A browse of curiosity brought to his attention that something was strange. Certain items seem to be out of their area, or not in their rightful place. Like where is the water trough, and when you did find one, where is the water at? I see no horses around. Where are the people and their livelihood at? The only thing I hear is the church bells ringing. As he pondered, he thought was that created by the winds or is someone underneath it as he heard jangling from the rope against its ball and twang.

Signaling something was out of context! Or perhaps there was a commission for a gathering.

When he studied the street, he entered the saloon called "Last Stop Saloon," he found nobody there, but cobwebs hanging off, of different items, just looming in the darkness. He thought to himself where is the woman that I thought I had seen in the window at?

But what he seen instead were cobwebs hanging off the legs of tables and chairs and even off walls and ceilings. There were no lights, but candles sitting in certain stands. And of course, they were unlighted.

While looking around the saloon and over and under the bar counter he found a suspicious covert as he opened the hidden suspicious drawer, he found a bottle of whiskey not opened yet. On its label was stamped the year 1877. The year I'm standing in is 1887! This bottle looked and said I'm Ten years old. As usual his thirst was unconceivable. His instinct and his pride- hood told him too, he had to open this bottle with gentleness to show he was a man in general. He thought to himself that he would be in this unusual query, a gentleman that showed respect. Even in his unclean worn-out clothes, he had to show some form of dignity and elegance. But he also thought that he needed to find some water for him and his horse.

For once he could smell the stench that came out from within his skin and inner clothes wear. This clavation of smelter didn't seem to bother him, for he was too tired to recognize it. The sounds were rhymical with a symbol of boldness, to which some were stunned by surprise.

As this man sat with a bottle of whiskey and got drunk on his own accord; he noticed before he nodded off, his time piece showed 12:00 noon. He fell asleep undisturbed with a half shot left in his glass and a bottle over two-thirds full. It felt like after an hour or two went by before he heard yelling and harassment in this once quiet bar.

And when he awoke, he noticed the saloon was alive with people. He had to shake his head a few times to make sure he wasn't dreaming again, some things were out of place, his mind started to go berserk. At least that's what he thought!

Wrong- way…. A repercussion of the past has shown itself.

An illusion came to ponder, as a saloon girl came up to him and asked if he needed a beer to wet his whistle. Didn't she notice the bottle of whiskey in front of him? Even the glass was half full. She smiled with dignity and seemed to be a little nervous about our acquaintance.

But when I looked down to the table the whiskey bottle and shot glass I had were gone! I glanced at my time piece, and it gazed back at me saying it was 12:01 pm. As our conversation slowed down, she was erupted by a strange man with no scruples. This big -ass farm boy wearing bib- overalls, looked as if he was over 300- lbs. of nothing their but, simplified stupidity. Me being a simple man was not even over 200- lbs. looked at him with hostility. I interrupted and asked the saloon gal for a bottle of whiskey, a glass of water and a shot glass. She said coming right up, as soon as I help this farmer out.

As he stood up looking mad at me, I got up too.

I laid my guns on the table, as he glanced at my eyes he said, sorry sir I didn't realize she was your gal. This man stood taller and bigger than I expected.

Why would he apologize to me? As I looked down to my guns with those pearly white- inscription's flowing along its grains, I wondered where did I picked them up at?

My pistols were usually wood barren handles with a few stains. I had no idea of killing people for a living! Or being a professional gun slinger, bounty-hunter, or perhaps some sort of a hunter of men in one form or another.

74

These people within glared at me with caution. It seems to me they were scared to death when they looked upon me. I glanced at myself, and I did notice between the men and bar maid they tried to keep their distanced, away from me.

I stood up and looked at myself in the mirror, over the bartender's counter, and what I seen was an image of a man with clean clothes suited with a white shirt and black leather vest. I glanced and thought about what is happening in this strange town, for this isn't me! Where did these clothes and guns come from?

I see more strangeness inside this saloon than I've ever seen outside in the streets, or even in the countryside that belongs to Mother-Nature. I did notice the Town came back to Life.

While I looked out of the windows and over the swinging saloon doors, I seen there were kids playing on the streets and horsemen trotting along the road, and there were horse and buggies with men and women steering the reins going down the road to their own destination. With little girls playing on the sides of buildings, playing house and nurses, with their little dolls., and little boys playing cowboys and Indians or sheriffs and bad men.

Of course, I seen them while I was standing by the swinging doors inside the saloon across the main roadway.

As I heard plagiarism coming from some of those, I noticed they chose upon themselves while others stood -up with absolute astonishment, and in some instances hatred; content was glowing, gazing from out of their eyes, my mind told me to hold still the substances that seemed to be on their very small mind.

Mind you, I'm flowing or gathering my wits from out of this sphere of its formidable reality that I seem to be caught in. I kept thinking please give me a break from this reality.

As I shook my head so gently, from side to side again with unbelief in this space of dreams. Then suddenly the saloon gal came back with a bottle of whiskey, a glass of water which I drank first, with a shot glass. The water tasted fabulous. As I started to pour whiskey in the shot glass, I was sipping on it carefully. The last time I was pouring and drinking shots down like there was no tomorrow.

The people in this bar were talking to one another as if they knew each other. There was one table where even a few were playing cards, I think it was poker as I heard faint sounds of coins rattling in the middle of the table board with raises and calls being announced. There was only one saloon gal taking care of the customers. And the owner was behind the bar.

The whiskey was going down smoother as I noticed that I was pouring myself shots at a faster rate. At least it felt that I was drinking them faster.

What I saw earlier was some hardcore cowboys and gamblers with a few drunkards looking for a free drink. But after a few drinks I went outside to glance at the people on the street, then suddenly it was empty. The washing of my memory was distinguished within my very soul. Some things have changed, but I'm still looking at it.

I had to bring my head up again from the table and look at my time piece again. The time didn't seem to switch…but it did say it was 12:01 noon.

I pondered to see if things will change again! The place was dirty and dry. My life seems to progress itself into a future adventure that I have no control over.

Delusion seems to be an adversary. As I wandered into the daydream, my sense has recognized there is a disruption of foul play. A proclamation dawned into my mind, what have I stumbled into?

As I went outside again standing on the boardwalk, I looked toward the east and then I faced the west, I asked myself loudly so where did the vision go? If anybody can answer my question, please let me know. Silence seems to be the prevalence.

So, have the winds caught up to you yet? Will this evasive force come haunting you even in your bed. As the winds come sailing across the sands and against the structures another force strikes with vigorous pain. You see yourselves in a distraught situation, asking yourself, will we come out alive?

I pushed the swinging saloon doors open to enter the bar room. The place was silent once again. I sat down where I sat before and opened the whiskey bottle to fill my glass, so I could get another drink. After four shots I laid my head down once again, lying my head down on the table. For tiredness has set in from all the traveling that I had done earlier, looking for a place to set my weary head.

*   *   *   *   *

The cowboy finds himself in an abandoned ghost town. But when he found this ten-year-old whiskey bottle unopened, he opened it and had a few drinks in the saloon and after taking a nap the town came back to life. One of the saloon girls came up to him, and it was the same gal that attended to him earlier asked would you like to wet your whistle with a drink cowboy? He thought the last time he hesitated to take anything, but this time he said to her, "could you bring me a whiskey bottle."

As he looked around the saloon there were cowboys gambling and drinking, supposedly having a typical time amusing themselves with discerning eyes.

As the saloon gal came back with a shot glass and whiskey bottle, she laid them on the table and walked away. Attending to other customers I noticed there were cowboys entering and a few had left.

This situation I found myself in was quite alarming, not knowing what to expect. When my eyes drifted down at my attire, I was wearing clean clothes with a bright white shirt and black vest. With those pearly white handle pistols on each side once again.

When the cowboy took out his time piece, for he was curious what time it was, it glared back at him and showed him it was 12:02 on its glass face. He thought to himself, surely that's not right, it must be later than that!

So, he put the time piece to his ear to make sure the watch was ticking as he jiggled it. Now this little episode caused his mind to wonder, what in the hell is going on inside this saloon!

For this watch was dependable and the most accurate time piece he ever owned or known. The pocket watch was a Zeitretter, known for its quality and accuracy and the price of it was not cheap either. And he always checked and wound it up each day. So, he decided to wind it up carefully before he stuck it back in his pocket. It only took one revolution to notice it was at the end near its springs.

While drinking the whiskey the bar gal gave him, he pondered hearing all the excitement that started at a table when one accused another of cheating. One of the gambling cowboys turned the table over and you could see all the money and cards spill to the floor. His eyes were glaring with hostile anger at the one he accused of cheating. As the ruckus got louder the saloon owner came over and told both there would be no fighting or gun playing in this joint, and if you can't settle it then take it outside on the street or in the alley.

The one being accused looked at the owner and the sidewinder who said he was cheating and gleamed at the accuser saying I'll meet you outdoors to settle this dispute, unless you're too yellow?

As he started through the swinging doors, he was looking back at the cowboy who accused him and the same sidewinder who turned over the table of drinks and poker money.

The crowd in the saloon were glancing at the man who charged the cowboy who just walked through the doors of cheating what he would do next.

He pondered, finally or seemly, getting his outburst of anger under control. But as he gazed at the faces of others, he could tell they wanted him to back up his claim. Since he made such a big commotion about dishonest card playing.

Then, the people in the saloon were expecting this cowboy they called Vernon to face Sonny, who he called a cheater. A face-to-face duel of some sort needed to take place.

As Vernon finally seen the predicament, he put himself in, he walked towards the swinging saloon doors heading outside on the street. After Vernon walked out looking a little shaky and disturbed everybody else rushed to the swinging saloon doors and proceeded outside also.

Sonny was waiting under the overhanging roof on the boardwalk of the saloon. While Sonny glanced at Vernon and said no one calls me a thief and cheater and thinks he can get away with it. He started to walk slowly onto the dusty road and that's when Vernon knew it was going to be a showdown.

As the crowd started to stand still and gather around getting out of the way, I proceeded through the swinging doors myself.

Then suddenly the scene went blank, and the town was empty once again as the whistling winds were blowing ever so hard and steady. I gazed rather curiously up and down the street, wondering what had just happened!

I went back into the saloon only to find it empty with cobwebs and dust settling all over the place. My whisky bottle I got from the saloon gal was gone along with the empty glass of water. The old whisky bottle that I've found earlier was back on the table and it still was almost 1/2 full, just sitting there. What was strange was it had disappeared when the saloon came back to life! And that was the time when the gal asked me if I wanted a drink.

I sat back down in the same place that I had originally sat in. The table was full of dust and cobwebs hanging from the table legs and chairs. I grabbed the bottle and poured me a shot, thinking about the events I witnessed in the bar.

While sipping from the shot glass I brought it to explore the rest of the saloon. The saloon gal had to get that glass of water I drank earlier someplace. As I roamed in the back, I found the kitchen full of dust and cobwebs looking the same as the tables in front. Nothing has changed except the design of the room. Some shelves above the counters were broken and hanging from their mounts on the wall.

I glanced at the sink where the water pump was located and found it was rusted and clogged up. As I looked at it carefully, I told myself that this pump hasn't worked in years.

After gazing inside this saloon with amazement, I went back to the same table and sat in the same chair and poured myself another shot of whiskey. I silently stared at the four walls of this room wondering what to do next. The only thing I had was this 10-year-old whiskey and a shot glass that I had found.

A despondent feeling overcame me, as I glared at this old whiskey bottle, pondering how this was happening. Once again after 5- shots I started to get droopy. My eyelids were secretly closing as I strained myself to keep them open. But eventually I laid my head on the table and fell asleep.

*   *   *   *   *

After about an hour went by, I heard noises and rambling in the saloon. When I woke up and glanced in front of me, I seen old and young cowboys in the saloon, drinking beer and whiskey and four of them were playing cards.

As I took my time piece out of my pocket, I noticed I was wearing a clean white shirt and had a black leather vest accenting a stunning appearance. I peered at the time piece, and it had the audacity to tell me it was 12:03 on its glistening glass. I watched the same waitress approaching me saying, hey cowboy, would you like to wet your whistle with a beer?

I looked at her and said, sure, but first do you have any water in this saloon? She glared at me, cockeyed and asked, why would you like to have a glass of water? And the cowboy gazed at the saloon girl and graciously said can I come with you? Now she advertently thought to herself, why would he want to come to the kitchen? Does he want to be alone with me? Or does he have something to say to me in private! When he finally persuaded her to take him, they got to the kitchen, he asked her where the water was coming from. She gasped and pondered, all you wanted to see is just the water pump and spicket!

Of course, the cowboy brought his beer with him as he went with the bar gal to the kitchen. The bartender asked where is that cowboy going? She told the owner that the cowboy wants to know where the water is coming from.

The bartender looked puzzled at the cowboy and said why not, and the cowboy mentioned he was interested in how the running water entered the building. After gazing at the water entry, he thought while looking at it, I saw this same spicket earlier and it was all clogged up and not functioning.

As I went back to the same table and chair, I started to drink a beer, but what I really wanted was a whiskey. So, I asked the waitress to bring me a bottle of bourbon whiskey.

I noticed once again that the 10-year-old whiskey bottle was missing from the table. I was puzzled, where was it going!

I needed to reminisce and collect my thoughts of what is happening and what I have learned within this town and saloon. After recollecting the repetition, he started to list them in his head. First, he thought after taking a nap from drinking whiskey from that old bottle, he would eventually be awoken by bystanders and laughable conversations or activities inside the saloon. Second, he noticed after he woke up from his stupor, the ten-year-old whiskey bottle had disappeared, and a saloon gal came up to him and always asked if he wanted a drink. Third, any time he left through the swinging doors of the saloon the town would turn back to its old deserted ghostly and windy appearance. The way he found it when he first entered the town and the saloon. In other words, the town appeared dead.

Another thing he couldn't figure out was his time piece wasn't keeping time right! At least that's what he thought. Each time he woke up from a drunken nap the time piece would show a one-minute increment under its glass caged seal.

This whole experience seemed rather odd and spooky. It was like the ghost of this town was coming back to life, but he was wondering what was triggering it, and what does it want from me? Who or what was allowing this town to come back to life after I had a sleepy or drunken nap? My thoughts got interrupted when an old cowboy looked at me and said, "I know you!"

I glared at the old gray-haired stranger and replied, "Where do you know me from?" I don't recognize you. While he squinted his eyes trying to get them focused on my disposition and my character, he happened to stumble, half-drunk as he seen the pearl handle pistols sticking out of the holsters I was wearing. He slightly bowed his head to me and apologized and said sorry sir I must be mistaken.

He wallowed away staggering and mumbling to himself as he approached the swinging doors, heading outside to gather his thoughts. I could slightly see him through the windows stumbling as he walked along the boardwalk. Disappearing out of sight. As I was up looking out of the window, I glanced out of the swinging saloon doors and as I peered over the door, I saw a boy was approaching alongside the building. He stopped when he heard shouting from someone down the road that I could not see. Anyways he turned back around and started walking again. As he approached the saloon door, I stopped the boy and asked him what his name was. He said Timothy. So, I asked Timothy if he wanted to make some money.

As we were talking with the doors between us, he gazed at me with those suspicious eyes, he said how much and what he would have to do.

About the time I was going to tell the boy, a farmer started walking towards the door in his bib overalls and shouted out to the guys in the bar that he needed to go to the feed store to pick up some items and look at his crops and his livestock. He mentioned that he wouldn't be back today. They shouted back to Freddy humorously joking don't work too hard for Gladys your little lady will expect that all the time. Freddy just smiled back as I got out of the way when he went through the doors. Timothy stood off to the side and apparently Freddy didn't notice him.

Freddy went off to the side of the building as he got on his horse and wagon while he moseys slowly down the street toward his destination. And when he was clearly gone, I spoke softly through the doors to ask Timothy if he was still there. He glandered under the doors and said I'm still here. I told him I have a shiny three- cent nickel here if you would check on my horse that's in the stable.

He looked and sounded puzzled; thinking isn't that Arnie's job the Livery owner's job. So, Timothy questioned me on this, and I told him I would feel better if someone just might check up on him, because he's a special horse. He said gee-whiz "OKAY" because it sure is worth a three-cent nickel to him.

I described to him that he was an Appaloosa sire, his name was "Shiner" and that he was white with spotted black marks with a ring around one of his eyes. I told Timothy to make sure he had water and some grain. And while you are at it fill up my two canteens with water and put them back on my dark saddle.

Before Timothy left, I asked him how much you think Arnie would charge me for him to give "Shiner" a rub down and the stall, grain? Timothy didn't know, so I handed him two-bits and told him to give it to Arnie. I asked Timothy if he had any problems, to come back and let me know. He said thanks mister for the money, while he started running up the road toward the Livery stable.

I decided to sit back and relax for a few minutes and sip on some whiskey. While the cowboys and farmers were at tables and bar stools telling stories to each other in pairs or small groups.

The next thing I know is that someone came walking through the doors with a six shooter on his side with a brown Stetson hat covering his head. There was a brown ribbon that was wrapped around the brim. When he came in the owner with some others were asking how the day was faring out. He calmly said with a steady voice that it appeared it was just an average of the mill day. The saloon keeper asked the sheriff if he wanted a beer. He looked at the bartender and said you don't have to ask me twice. For I believe it's going to be a scorcher. Someone barked out and said it's already hot enough to cook an egg on a frying pan without a fire.

I discreetly glanced at his pistol and thought that it didn't look special. Just an ordinary type with an oak handle, probably a colt .38 army revolver. But then again in 1877 that was a good pistol alongside a Smith & Wesson. As I looked down at those pearl white handle pistols, I was wearing they appeared to be .41 calibers, slightly stronger than his. But both were powerful enough to knock a man down to where he couldn't get back up, if you hit him in the right place.

Drinking shots at a time silently by myself, I started to get a little blurry from my eyesight. Suddenly I heard someone coming through the doors of the saloon shouting out to Samuel come quickly we're having problems at the Livery stable. Immediately I shook my head saying to myself, that's where "Shiner" is! When I saw the sheriff with two others following the man who shouted, I frantically followed without thinking, that as soon as I went through those doors out across the boardwalk onto the road that the town went dead.

Once again, the old winds were blowing and the dust from the road was flying. It appears I was standing in a ghostly, haunted town.

I thought while I'm at it that I'll go to the Livery stable to see what all the outcry was about.

While walking to the stable I heard the bells ringing from the church. As I was walking with my back against the wind, this was when a strange thought came to me about that bell. Why didn't the pastor of the church or someone else take that bell with them! While it was blaring out plunks of twinges from the sounds of metal pounding each other I thought the rope must of dislodged from the rope hitch, causing it to twang from the rustling wind.

When I finally got there, I opened the swinging barn doors as the wind kept sailing even inside the barn. I took the props out from the doors and the wind forced the doors to close. I seen "Shiner standing there with no delight left. But it looked like he wasn't thirsty or hungry, and I thought maybe if I'm in that saloon and the town comes back to life that there is water and food. I was a little confused at that point.

I decided to gaze around in this dusty, dirty barn that appears to have slatted planks on the side of the building and ins between the slats is gaps one inch or more in widths. And in the corner, it looks as though there was an office where the owner kept his books and ledgers. And against the shelves was a bench with some drawers underneath it, but they were damaged up. On the top of the bench, he seen small, opened coverts where the owner apparently kept smaller articles at. And off to the left of the bench table he seen two-bits and a shiny three-cent nickel.

I pondered about it as I was talking to myself loudly, asking Shiner to come over here and said to him, do you know anything about this? He shook his head up and down and started to prance around. I scratched the side of my head in bewilderment, wondering, surely this isn't the same money I gave to the boy, is it!

I was debating to myself if I should put the money back in my pocket, then I thought let it just sit here, for they are taking care of you aren't they Shiner. He let out a gentile whine when I said that. I looked carefully at him, and he appeared to be healthy and fed.

When I was about to leave, I told Shiner that I would be back. Out of the corner of my eye I have seen two canteens on my saddle with my nap sack and bags sitting on a rickety stall fence. Well, that's where I put it when I started to explore the town and saloon. I got to thinking there have been some weird things going on, so I'll check out these canteens.

As I unscrewed one of the caps on my beaver skin metal canteen, I poured some into my hand expecting some water. And what I got was sand. When I checked the second canteen it was full of sand also. I poured the sand out of both canteens and straddled them back to the saddle. It appears that when this town dies, everything goes back to its formal originality.

So, now I know that I can never take anything from this town when I decide to leave. And I presume if I leave anything here, it will sit on a table or someplace else and just collect dust or rust. I glared at Shiner and stated to him like I was talking to another person saying, what did we get ourselves into! He let out a sneer like he understood me. When I looked at my watch it showed on its bald face glass that it was 12:04 in the afternoon. I thought when I saw that, that it was a lie.

I started back to the saloon after I said goodbye to Shiner. When I reached the saloon through that blistering wind, I proceeded into the bar room with nothing there but spider webs and dust. But on that familiar table sat the old whiskey bottle almost a ¼ full, with three chairs lodged around it. The same table chair set up and the same bottle with an empty shot glass staring at me in the face. After sitting down, I pulled the cork out of the bottle and poured a shot and drank it quickly. Filled up another and drank it as fast as I drank the first one. I did the same thing two more times before relaxing.

Staring through the musky stale air toward the darken walls I just saw a reflection of life. It seemed a mist was just floating as I was pouring myself more shots after another.

This crazy dimension that I find myself in has me speculating on what is going to come next. Can not leave the saloon without the town turning into a ghost settling dust bowl. With no life, no water, no food, just a haunted resemblance of ghostly spirits that are stuck into a realm of supernatural events.

These were my thoughts while sipping now from this old whiskey bottle. As my mind just pondered from one thing to another,

I felt delusional and I'm witnessing my eyes once again are getting heavy from being saddened. While looking intently at the bottle it glanced back at me stating that it was almost gone. Maybe a shot or two was left. My heavy head slowly laid its weariness on the table, and I passed out from exhaustion.

All you seen was a cowboy in a dusty old, abandoned saloon snoring away with his head on a table waiting for a ruckus to come in to wake him up. It seemed like two- hours had passed before cowboys and farmers were drinking and having a good time-sharing story after story and some of their daily run ends. I woke up over the commotion and a saloon gal came up to me and asked if I wanted to wet my whistle. I told her yes; do you serve steak? She said, "the biggest steak" in the county. Okay then I'll take a beer, a glass of water and a great big fat medium- rare steak with onions. She said coming right up.

I reached down to look at my time piece and its hands were pointing to the 12;05 position from its sparkling glass. I told myself the time is still wrong.

The bar gal brought out the beer and water and said the steak would be ready in five minutes. I started sipping on the beer as I glanced at the surroundings in the saloon. I decided when I'm done, I'll leave this place and I'll probably never see it again.

The waitress came out with the steak and asked if there would be anything else. I replied no thanks this should do. As she left, she was getting orders from other people. Mostly cow pokes and the likes. When I finished, she gave me a tab on a blank tablet of paper stating I owed $1.00 for the steak and a nickel for the beer. So, I gave her a dollar and two- bits and told her to keep the change. She thanked me as I left the saloon.

Then the town became silent once again with only the bell ringing and the wind gushing through the center of town. I picked up "Shiner my horse" and rode out of town. I decided to go up on top of a hill where I turned back around, and watched the town disappear before our very eyes. You could not tell if anything was ever there. I reached for my time- piece, and I could hear the ticks, as its fingers pointed to 12:06 this afternoon.

SHORT BREATH OF THE STORY

The title of story is: *A Winter Coldness Appears.* This is about a place just north of the Artic Circle, possible Norway. This man lives in a cold region where he has wood heat and uses huskies to drive his sleigh to town for provisions. After loading wood in his fireplace, he fell asleep. When he woke up, he heard noises outside and his dogs were howling and whimpering. He found his best male dog shot to death. He left his dogs penned up so they wouldn't follow him. He seen sled shoe tracks leading out from his house and he got his rifle and gun and started following these tracks. The female dog got out when he was about 2-miles from the house. Together they found the man who shot his dog. Now the story will tell the names of characters and dogs, and the consequences the man faces from the results of his actions.

A Winter Coldness Appears

As a man gazed in the wilderness, he saw a somberness of winter approaching, his first instinct told him to begin, getting ready for a cold season. As the trailing winds were forming, seeing the snow falling from the sky in a gusting spurious agony, he seen flakes bigger than his fingers were. Oh my, was his first impression, he noticed how the father of winter has sprung upon the mountainside, as his thoughts started to wonder. Mind you we are still in November, a month before winter even starts. It was Thursday November 20th. While the cool breeze was blowing continually against his face and skin, you wonder if this is a test to acknowledge your capability. He pondered on this distraction!

While the chilling winds and snow were spraying its display, his huskies were in the shed with straw and hay, lying down in some comfort zone. He had 6- huskies for his sled. Three - females and three- males. Six more were just recently born, eight -weeks back. These animals loved the snow. The mother was in the stage of weaning them from herself, so they had to be adjusted to feeding themselves.

This was typical in this region for coldness and snow was part of the topographical arena. They would provide travel to town for provisions and trade. Besides they liked to run in the snow. This was a natural tradition that started from years back.

Of course, some masters locked and mistreated their dogs to oblivion. When not needed these dogs were locked somewhat into chains into the elements of snow and blizzards from poor masters who didn't have shelters; or could care less of them.

Others at least had dog houses and let the dogs make a choice. Sometimes these dogs liked the outside area, still others would like some shelter from time to time.

These we called tyrants of poor judgement. For there was no law of cruelty amongst animals of any nature. Those who judge carelessly we denounced them on all levels of humanity. From those who cared about them put them into lean- to type sheds for adequate shelter for their homelife.

For there was a season to build adequate shelter. A journeyman had a certain compassion for his dogs who would risk themselves for his salvation.

Still others had no compassion on this matter, but insisted they were nothing but slaves who had four- legs.

Some individuals held his dogs with utmost respect of where he kept them; he used a gate and put forth a rope or chain, keeping them inside this barren they called home. Of course, he would feed these dogs at least twice a day with some form of rationing. Water was plentiful from the snow and ice.

And of course, in most places there was a continual water flowing down a small creek bed, that spread out in different formations.

This formation of snow and ice started to proceed the beginning of a nightfall of coolness as temperatures began dropping in the single digits. The windfalls were making it harder to establish its abrasions of temperatures. The gloominess of darkness proceeded, as the skies above shown an estrange flow of clouds above with different colors after the snow would cease a few hours before; this glowing spectacular beauty along the horizon as it was approaching, it was showing off a fascinating of wonderment. This insightful man with his shiny eyes were sparkling at this unusual arrangement, with thoughtfulness...

A distinguishing symbol along the coloring sky seemed to show a picture of elegant pictorials of images dashing across the skies above. It seems to have seen different formations from the animal kingdoms. His mind inquired am I being exhausted into an episode of hypnotism, but what was he thinking about, was another question? His imagination started to go from here to whatever's! But what did he acknowledge from its beauty.

As the science of climate grew, there was no explanation of when the weather changed. He did notice the dogs in the pen were starting to get a little anise; in there penned up allocation and surroundings.

They looked unusually on edge, while being secluded in a fenced -up barrier. But this shelter was comfortable, and these dogs loved it. From what he observed it didn't seem to bother him at the time.

There were times he would allow the dogs to roam with the pinned unlocked, usually three times a week. They could stretch their legs and muscles and run for sporting events. These animals needed exercise to be efficient. While he let them go wandering in this rough terrain of snow, he realized their adventure was showing compassion from one to another. They were playing like kids who saw snow for the first time. These dogs were playing amongst themselves in a free atmosphere of solitude.

There were no strangers around or presence of anything unusual, these guys were even having fun along with their master. As the sun started to swallow itself up in the west, he seen the darkness approaching from the east, wondering what this night might bring forth. As he put his dogs back up in the stable, he pondered, the days are getting somewhat shorter. This unique man with his unusual constraint, was wiggling a formal thought, as he spoke, let the night bewilder itself on its own conclusion. Then he started thinking, what does that mean? He thought of his ancestry. And his friends gave him a warning. Of course, this is from years back, when he was innocent and wet behind the ears.

The image from years back showed where he came from.

While the night progressed into simplicity a frowning disturbance was forming on the outskirts of his home. As he was sticking more firewood in his fireplace and chimney, he thought this was a good time to sleep. Fallen asleep in front of his own fireplace and as quiet as the crackling wood would cry, anointing itself with cries of sheer agony it would send sounds of hysteria. But then again it would send heat to comfort him and his home. Oh my, have we lost compassion even upon our friends!

A transpiring analogy was introduced along with his nighttime dream. He started to shiver even with the warmth of the fireplace. To his astonishment even his dream made him wonder, should we cry or weep! Suddenly, he woke from out of his stupor and heard a noise outside of his house. The dogs started barking, embarking there was something outside that they were not use too. During this yelping of the dogs yapping in the locked-up constriction they were enclosed in; sent strange sounds to the owner of his property and especially to his dogs.

As he dragged his feet to the white formation of snow on his front porch, in which there was probably at this time more than 10- inches on the ground. He looked around to see if something was suspicious. He had a hard time opening his front door with all the white-powdering icy sustenance hanging off his door jamb.

He started to put his best winter clothes on, with his best snow- shoe boots. He also brought his rifle with him. A fallen cry he heard from his doorstep when his dogs started yelping in pain. As he approached the shelter of his dogs, he found one lying on the ground with a red tainted stain encircling the dog's chest area, as he lay there in stillness.

A dog has been shot! There was a yelping noise and pain coming from the penned-up dogs. He took his rifle out with him and thought who would shoot a penned-up dog? Why didn't he hear a sound of gunfire? Was it because of the storm with all its snow pounding upon him, or was it because he was so tired? As he looked at the dog, his heart went out to the rest saying, I'm so sorry to see Earl go out like this. For this dog was the commander in chief. His dominance was short of breath- taking. Being in his presence was commendable. He was a leader of most dogs, and they knew it.

That's what he called his first dog for defense in this regime of traveling dogs. This dog weighed 110-lbs and stood 3 foot tall from his back to his paws on the ground and was solid as a rock. He was also the protector for his domain. Currently, it was Friday November 21[first]. He decided to get his medical kit. Knowing that Earl was dead, he proceeded to pull the bullet out of his chest, so he could examine it. He found out it was from a rifle, aka, maybe a Mauser G33/40 rifle or Mauser 8mm carbine. He thought to himself, who carries 8mm or perhaps 11.25 mm bullets? Depends on the rifle! But who carries them? But then again what is the diameter of the bullet in question. Jeremiah at this point, cried., and was worried.

The sadness brought all the other pups together to hover over their former father. As Jeremiah hovered and cradled over one of his best friends, he relinquished his crying. Sympathy was a display along with the other animals and dogs. Earl was a lifeline of security. He hugged the other dogs gracefully while gathering each one independently as he cried one to another.

Their glowing bluish and greenish eyes stared continually at him and their father of dogs. Earl was so still they howled with a murmuring low-key sadness over his departure. He wondered why you would do such a thing as killing a dog penned upped. He looked contently at the area of this shed and barn, wondering who was here? Evidently, he must have shot through the gates as the outer door was open. He asked his dogs where is the perpetrator at?

They barked and glanced out into the snow, and he seen some form of tracks. This individual was wearing mid- size snowshoes. The ones you strapped to your boots. He noticed these snowshoes were not normal. Perhaps from some form of an organization or perhaps a club. So, he decided to get his snowshoes and follow this track he left behind him. Of course, he brought his Mauser G33/40 wood grain 11.25 mm rifle, with extra shells, and thought this would be adequate in case he ran into a confrontation. His biggest contortion of equalization was something he inquired from years back. He shunned thinking that a local villager would do such a thing. But with more investigation he noticed this was outside his parameter. He decided to make it simple.

He also brought an M/1914 pistol in a belt type holster with extra shells, it was compared to a .45 Army brand military pistol on all fronts. As he pondered about his dogs, he decided to leave his friends behind for a reason. He didn't want any more unnecessary animals being killed.

It broke his heart when he heard his dogs whimpering from this unnecessary atrocity, that man who shot Earl unnervingly, has he got hatred stuck inside himself without any sense of remorse. This brought a passion of unity to this household, where the dogs looked contently at their master.

As he was gathering his provisions, he thought maybe he would bring some drinking water and food. As he followed the tracks in his snowshoes this adventure started to be a little longer than he thought.

The snow fell faster than what he expected. There were quarter size increments of snowflakes dropping faster than he could see. He had doubts about finding this perpetrator.

Even sleet began falling from these dew type clouds. A man needed a face mask with some form of warmth. He was happy he brought his best boots and gloves with head warming apparel.

While the snow started collecting faster than he could walk. Oh my, he kept repeating to himself, oh my gosh, was another form of aggravation when he glanced to the ground. His sound from his inner's body doesn't know if I can reach him!

The temperatures dropped to minus -15 degrees during the evening. He could barely see the trace in the snow as the moonlight was momentarily peeking through the clouds and snow trying to shine its brightness.

The pines and oak were whistling a silent breeze with nothing there but stillness edging itself against the cones on the ground and leftover dried up branches from oak trees. Gee came out of his mouth wondering if we will make any progress from this trip.

While traveling in the snow bound landscape and darkness approaching, it was time to find a place to set up a campsite. Besides he was getting a little tired.

It was time to stop and rest, he thought as his breath was exhaling strong breaths of air and puffy white smoke to gain his strength and gather some wood and start a fire to heat himself from this frigid coldness. It was time to rest as he went looking for the trail. At this time, he notices and seen Sheba the female husky there looking at him with a smile. He glanced at her and said, "What are you doing here?" The husky gazed at him as she was happy, she found him in this coldness. He looked at her and thought, I'm happy to see you too. How did you get out of the pen?

She just looked at him with those glistening greenish-bluish eyes, that seem to penetrate you with sincerity. So, they spent the night together around the campfire in homage.

The only thing he brought for food was beef jerky and a canteen of water. As morning and daylight formed it was Saturday November 22nd, he seen the mark that he laid out the day before; before it got covered up from the snow. As this was gradually falling from the sky above. He proceeded traveling into a stillness of snow, his breath was forming exhales of huge particles coming out through his mouth and nostrils.

This man could see a coolness of whiteness coming out of Sheba's mouth, but it seems she had better breath than what he had. In other words, she could tackle the cold better than he could even think about.

She would respond and look at him directly for an instant just to see how he was doing. There he noticed and seen formations of some slush, squishing past his boots as he proceeded and went another mile; it seemed it took him a few hours to get where we were supposed to follow, wondering, as they went along pondering, if we'll see this man from our house and homestead again? Sheba knew we were on the right trail, as she would inform him, with suggestions from her insinuations.

While the man stopped again as the sun was starting to diminish against the top half of trees and sky, he acknowledged to Sheba he was tired; let's set-up camp, Sheba was so agitated when she started jumping up and down and crying with empathy, saying we are so close to the perpetrator, that she could smell him.

But Jeremiah told Sheba while grasping her furry neck looking into her eyes, saying, glance upwards I see no smoke in the sky. Therefore, this individual is cold. Let us, let him freeze. We will get him tomorrow at daybreak.

As Jeremiah spread out the deep snow to make a firewall, like he did last night, he retrieved small oak and pine branches to start a fire. And with pine it started quickly. Again, there was warmth that he could warm his hands and feet with. As he tried to calm Sheba, she went out adventuring. After a while he got so tired that he started to fall asleep in this embodiment of warmth, especially when he was wrapped in a blanket and there was extra wood sitting off to the side.

As early dawn came unannounced, in which it was November Sunday the 23rd, Sheba came up and started licking his face. There were still branches of pine and oak still sitting there, but the fire was getting low. I looked at her and said, why did you wake me up? She just grinned and jumped up and down pointing to me the direction, the man was seen last.

I glanced at her with a serious gaze and told her I already knew. But let him freeze for a while. While walking in this drudging snow allowing several hours to slide by, wondering if we would catch up to this villain as more hours came and went; I could tell that Sheba and I were getting tired.

After several hours we came up to a dried-up rocky creek bed. There was a dried-up bank of snow lying there with frozen stagnated water. And across, just on the other bank lay a dark object.

A man with frozen hands, icicle's hanging off his beard. Snowshoes dappling off his feet. And there was a rifle lying beside him. It appeared he just froze to death! He must have been there several hours barely shivering in this climate of below zero. He was turning into an icicle.

Sheba growled at him with content, knowing he shot Earl her mate in cold blood. Jeremiah had to hold her back.

Apparently, he was still alive, and we tried shaking him, to possibly rejuvenate him from his suffering, but he kept reaching for his rifle. It was though he wanted to shoot me or Sheba. But his hands could not hold on to his rifle.

Jeremiah asked him a direct question; did you shoot my dog that was locked in my pen? And if so, why? His voice could barely speak. His mouth was closing off from the coolness of freezing itself from the ever so coldness the winds were blowing.

In other words, this man was starting to freeze to death. But for some reason or another we didn't feel sorry for him. Besides he tried to pull his rifle on us.

He looked carefully at the man, then we gazed at Sheba the husky, wondering what shall we do? He asked the man who couldn't talk right, what is your name?

When he couldn't mumble a word, from his frozen mouth and tongue, Jeremiah decided to start a campfire so they could all get heated up from this minus -15 degrees. It took several hours to get this campfire going in a positive direction. Sheba always kept a strong eye on this perpetrator, constantly engaging a strict sense of foulness.

The man could sense this dog wanted to tear him in pieces, and we were the only one's holding her back. In other words, she was angry.

Several times we had to coax Sheba, be patient. Settled down, he will see justice, one way or another. But the glare she gave with those eyes could scare some of my best friends. The penetration with her eyes and demeanor had him spooked. I told him we only had to glance one way or another and she'll have your Adam's apple for comfort.

She constantly showed her teeth in some form of hatred toward this man. She knew who shot and killed Earl her betrothed. It didn't take much studying on this matter.

As I collectively gather the wood and tried to start a flame in a secluded breech, the atmosphere seemed to acknowledge the wind wanted to blow harder than expected. This man was shaken from his teeth down to his limbs. Ice was forming, even in his hair. He was shaking constantly. The temperature dropped another degree or two, as the sun started to peek against the western sky, behind the forest of unsuspected trees.

As I collectively gathered the kindle and branches to start a fire, Sheba was guarding the prisoner very closely. The darken clouds began to proceed above, with a glistening color of reddish blueness, with orangish- yellowish streaks forming across the horizon and there were other assorted figments of unusual colorization presenting itself. A purplish color also presented a figment of attraction.

The winds decided to denounce the blow it had earlier. The fire began to lighten the campsite with some form of warmth. But it seems you had to be right next to it, to get any benefit from its wonder. As the smokey moisture of its foliage was spreading through a condensed smothering of smoke you couldn't stay too close to the fire. Or it would choke you from breathing right. A severe fire had to brighten the flames with constant heat, without you gasping for relief.

As Jeremiah added more sticks and some small size logs the fire was tracing itself above the trees to the above limits. Suddenly flames were being noticed from the campfire. You could see bluish-red and purplish flames with their yellow tips spewing a natural heat source, while sitting around it. It took over three hours to get to this point.

Of course, he had to get more logs, so he could put them close to the fire, so he could dry them out. Looking contently at these logs you seen moisture dripping out of their porous bark and skins, while he was continually putting mid-size branches on its fire. In cold weather like this a campfire needed a continuous feeding of wood on its firepit. Or it would eventually go out and you would have to start it again, especially when you hadn't collected any coals of ashes yet.

As the fire got to the point of putting some heat in the area, we all straddled near the firepit, while sitting close enough to it as possible, there was movement amongst those who had freezing limbs and legs. Especially the toes and fingers were somewhat frostbitten.

As everyone was getting somewhat hungry and thirsty, you could see eyes looking at each other. Jeremiah sat there with sincerity, in his tone, he proceeded to take out his parcel, saying with a gesture to each one, saying I don't have much, and gave them a healthy stick of jerky. He hands feed Sheba, so, she wouldn't gobble it up in one gulp. As he took his canteen, in which it was frozen and placed it over the fire carefully, they shared the water when it changed its solid to a slushy liquid.

As the temperatures were dropping once again, it seemed we were huddling the firepit even closer. Jeremiah was consistently throwing wood on the fireplace. Wood was burning faster than he could haul it in. As the perpetrator got warmer, he suggested you go and get some wood, as I have my pistol on you and Sheba will watch your every movement. The man started to rebuttal, but he knew there wasn't any cause for it because he was freezing within himself. Someone needed to get more firewood.

As the firewood was depleting in this certain area. They had to venture further out. Then the coolness of the winds and breeze took our breath away. The temperatures had fallen another 5 degrees. It felt like minus -30 degrees forming across our coats and skin. Luckily there was enough heat to keep you from freezing, but not warm enough to sleep.

I thought to myself, "is this the end of November! But no, it's only November 24th on a Monday. We haven't started winter yet! Hearing the footsteps and gruntled of the man with a load of wood in his hands, Sheba was right behind him watching his every move. He brought the wood and threw it on the ground, close to the firepit. Cursing the actions and process of searching for wood, from an empty forest and field. This was not an easy task.

Concerning the heat, we kept the fire going as you seen eyelids fluttering, but Jeremiah kept pressuring the strange man, about his identity. Even Sheba would not let loose the intensity that was in her blood boiled system.

Finally, the man spoke up; he was an escape convict from a prison. His name, according to what he claimed, addressed his name as Louie Saponite. I guess it was Italian, or perhaps Greek. Don't know for he would not suggest anything further.

But Jeremiah looked closely at his rifle and inquired to the man, isn't this a Mauser G33/40 rifle that carries an 8mm or perhaps a 11.25 bullet? He kept quiet about the rifle and wouldn't denounce it or suggest anything about it. As Jeremiah took the rifle and started to unload the shells, he found them to be an 8mm rifle. He questioned him, asking why did you kill my dog? I hope you can give me a legitimate answer. Or perhaps I may kill you in the same format. He looked closely at this stranger when he made his case. Sheba was staring very closely about anything that proceeded out his mouth and his demeanor. She had more common sense than I did.

As the stranger seen the seriousness of his consequences, he would just suggest bits and pieces of his actions. I asked with sincerity where did you get this rifle from? He said I took it from a guard that I overpowered. Me and two others broke out at the Norwegian penitentiary prison. This region was above the Arctic circle. There was only one prison in this district. After that he wouldn't say anything more. He said I already know I'm doomed.

When morning approached Jeremiah with Sheba said to Louie the stranger it's time to go back home. The man asked what are you going to do with me? Jeremiah looked at him and frowned, I don't know yet.

The climate was unexpected, at times with swirling winds gusting across the wooded terrain. If or when the snow fell, you had to go slow and make your own paths, in order to use your dogs and sleigh. He could tell this man's hands and feet were still cold as icebergs as he gently walked very carefully across the dreaded snow, as there was ice that was formed underneath and hiding itself from those who were on the surface.

As I looked ahead and seen this man struggling with his footing and pain was forming on his face, I thought let's take a 10-minute break. While taking a sip of water, our tongues got to loosen up, and I asked, so where are your partners at? He dazed into the field and sky, pondering, saying either they eluded the establishment or been captured.

I have no clue, because we decided at the beginning to choose our own paths. We thought we would let the authorities choose one path and we had three different paths to follow, from our own plans.

Jeremiah glared at him and said, "Did you choose wisely your path? Evidently not, said the stranger while calling himself Louie, he said I was unprepared from this outbreak of coldness, it hit me, and I found myself ready to die, until you saved me.

Jeremiah looked contently at him and said, "I haven't saved you yet! As his eyes looked sternly at his adversary along with Sheba his loyal dog. He reminded Louie, you still haven't answered my question. He glanced at me with a quizzical look. He asked what question was that?

Why did you shoot my dog? His name was Earl. He has been faithful to me for seven- years. Sheba here was his mate. So why did you?

As the man's eyes glared at Sheba and then toward the opened fields of snow, he started to describe what happen a few days back, during that mid- afternoon. He started out by saying, as I approached, I noticed your house cabin. And when I walked by the entry of the shed, a big dog started barking and growling and he caught me by surprise. I suddenly turned towards him with my finger on the trigger and pulled it; before I realized he was fenced in. When I saw him fall and whimper, I got scared. So, I ran into the woods, hoping that I could get away, before anybody seen me. Jeremiah gazed at him and said, "See what happens when you are scared and hysterically unbalanced. You lose sight of morals, and better judgement.

They started walking again, this time at a slower pace, for tiredness had set in. Jeremiah said let's set up camp again. Get some wood Louie, and you keep an eye on him Sheba. Jeremiah cleared out a bare spot to form a fire from the ground, so the snow and ice would not affect the dryness of the kindling.

As they got closer to home, Jeremiah stopped. He reached out to Louie Saponite and said, since it's close to our holidays. I'll give you a choice. Temperatures were still huddling around zero degrees.

Jeremiah said, either one thing or another; I can take you back to prison.... Or I give you to Sheba.... Or I'll set you free... He cried set me free.... I said is that what you want... he kept shouting set me free... I told him, are you sure you want freedom?

He said there are stipulations on freedom! He shouted nothing. Anything.

I told him strip your clothes off to your long underwear.

2nd take your boots off. 3rd. run faster than Sheba can, I'll give you a 1-hour head start. If you pass, then you will have your freedom. I insinuated, start running.

Louie looked cautiously at him and said, how can I survive with nothing on, plus not even a knife to defend myself? Jeremiah glared at him, those are the terms; take it or we'll proceed to taking you to the constable and surely you will go back to prison. Louie just shook his head with doubts and started running faster than what I expected.

Of course, I knew the temperatures would drop again tonight with another 6" of snow being sensed. The clouds of the sky loomed with a wintery fog. I told myself, either Sheba gets him, or this man will freeze to death, and I knew it. Is that justice. I should hope so. Within 3- hours I heard screams of agony beyond the hills and streams that were presented along the woods. Who was it from, I could only speculate. Sheba came back with satisfaction.

SHORT BREATH OF THE STORY

An Innocent Man is the name of this story. Cecil is the main character, and he lives as a hobo in Dublin, Ireland. The year was 1825, the provisions were low and most of the people were poor. The vicinity he is near would be off the Liffey River near Ha' Penny pedestrian bridge. Close by there is a somewhat mission feeding homeless soup in the evening.

Cecil was stuck in a trap when there were two murders that was committed, that he was close by, when they occurred on O' Connell Street and Eden Quay. He goes through a series of people doubting his innocence. It goes all the way up to the criminal courts in Dublin.

AN INNOCENT MAN

A violent rage of anger was trailing alongside and was a part of his character. As the man went inside to help gather his senses and try to put his mind into focus a loudness was interrupting his quiet zone. As the noise was starting to subside somewhat, he started to relax again. As he looked around, he found himself in a big room with a divider and a 1-table pool room with pictures of its country men and its famous landlords with landscape in the background setting up on the walls. Now the activity started to get rile up again as pints of beer and ale were being passed around that was bought from customers.

Most of them were daily consumers coming in at a nightly rate. Some were even coming in during the afternoon hours. It looked as though the bartender was laughing it up as his disgusting voice looked as though it hadn't been washed or cleaned for a while. He probably didn't realize that they came out with toothbrushes yet while enjoying the discussions being presented across the lengthy barroom counter that others were also laughing and enjoying their stories and jokes.

No one seemed to notice the man who enter just a few minutes ago. His frailty and lonely outward behavior appeared contrite as he moved ever so slowly. Wearing this old black attire wasn't giving him any special treatment from others. When he walked in, just taking a few steps, he saw a stool to sit on and it was sitting right next to the door against the wall of this so-called Pub. His demeanor and stature weren't noticed in the least. It appeared they could care less. This little palace was originally set up to get away from the stress of the day, the job, and especially the nagging wives. This here was a man- cave, so they boasted to each other, while they knocked their glasses together.

Eventually the timid but angry man walked up to ask the owner of this here Dive for a glass of water. He replied, go wet your whistle someplace else, or order a fermented ale to wash down your thirst. He glanced at him, being rather puzzled and said what would it hurt to wash down my thirst with a glass of water. Those around who heard this clapped with excitement at the sullen man and told him you have some brass to talk to Waldo like that.

And when they laughed, they implied to Waldo as a big chump letting a little harmless long-length dwarf like that to give him orders, particularly in his own Public House. Now after the riling of the customers already having a good time quarreling with one and another, the man with black abused attire gazed at Waldo with sincerity, expecting a glass of water. Waldo looked at him and with a timbering voice said, are you still standing in front of my bar? I only allow friends and paying customers to stand there while contributing funny amusement and stories. His jaw dropped and told him you're neither; so, buzz off. As he looked at his buddies, they all cheered him on and the others were shouting be off with you, you old scallywag.

Now Cecil was his name and he turned to head for the door then he turned back around to say, I'll remember this you uppity up heathens. As they laughed whole heartily when he went through the door, he glanced at the blackened sky and street, wondering which direction to head in too. He didn't want to go back home to his abandoned broken-down abode just yet. For in Ireland as poor as the streets were, it was tough to go home broke without anything but those smelly clothes you have on your back. Besides he would have to cross over the bridge, and they wanted you to pay a toll charge in order to cross Liffey River.

This small narrow walkway for pedestrians, they called a bridge, was given the name Ha' Penny. For it would cost you a half-cent, levy tax. But in 1825 it was hard to come across any sort of money, unless you had some form of employment. He thought let's go to the soup kitchen on the way and see if I haven't used my weekly tickets up just yet. For when Cecil searched his pockets, he couldn't find a spare ticket. It appears he's used up his weekly expended. Now as Cecil was walking towards the homeless shelter off from O' Connell Street, and he had to go on Ormand Quay he was thinking about how he is going to explain or other words lie to the doorman so, he could enter and get a bowl of watery potato and usually chopped onion soup.

And as he was heading towards the soup kitchen, he ran into one of his roommates. It was Abner walking towards the same place. He asked Abner, where have you been? As Abner looked at him, he mentioned that he was walking along Ormond Quay Lower Street. He told me that it was as dry as a bone and even the fishermen were broke. While I grinned at him, I inquired, did you have any luck finding anything else but water down potato soup.

Abner said that's where he's heading. Cecil rather glanced at Abner and just mumbled no luck where I went. At Waldo's Pub I couldn't even get a drink of water before they ran me out.

While they stood there talking with one another Cecil brought up the situation of a free pass for soup at the palace kitchen. Then he grinned.

Abner looked at him kind of sheepish and shrugged I've ran out this week hoping they may give me an advance for next week. Cecil thought, well, we can try it together, but you know how strict they can get, if they feel someone is taking advantage of their system, they will put us outdoors. Remember they say only four- times a week can you have this benefit. And they escorted me outside a few times trying the same thing you're talking about, and told me to wait until your tickets resume, then you can have a bowl of soup.

While I was describing this routine to the space of air and Abner was listening, I was scrutinizing it as I proceeded to start at the beginning of what someone would have to go through before they qualified, and I called it demeaning. As they handed out tickets on a Sunday after the preacher says some words about redemption. Then we sang some psalms and then we got in a line for our free four- tickets and Sunday doesn't count for getting a bowl of water down potato and onion soup.

Abner was gazing and he made the comment, Aye, sounds like this is the life for poor guys like us doesn't it, Cecil. Cecil glared at him thinking he may have a mental problem. As the two of them approached the mission of Brotherly Love the man at the door asked us for our ticket. I quaintly said now sir, we have momentarily lost our last ticket when a ruckus of boys overcame us and stole what we had in our pockets. The doorman looked at them with doubts in his mind and said, where did this all happened and when. Well Cecil piped up further since he started these lies and pointed over the bridge on the other side.

He described this unpleasant scene with saddened eyes, and when he glanced over and seen Abner looking suspicious, he kicked Abner on the shin and said wasn't it Abner. A terrible scene, shouted Abner. And the doorman said, exactly what did they do! Abner looked attentively at me, thinking I would have all the answers. I told the man, well see, visualize this; Whilst we were walking as cheerful as we possible could, that out of the dark it seems like a half dozen hoodlums came rushing out and had us cornered and told us to give it up.

The doorman looked at both of us as Abner was staring into the sky looking as guilty as sin, and me standing there with my face glooming towards his feet. He stared at us and asked, "is this all of your story" or is there more you need to tell me. Abner frantically glared at me with those worried eyes. I nodded my head and squinted with an up and down motion of my face, saying yea sir.

As skittishly as we appeared he motioned to go on in, but don't make it a habit. Next time I won't be so generous to you two bums. We hurriedly walked in and stood in line for a bowl of hot water with some onion and potato flavor, and thankful we got that. Tonight, there was some portion of stale bread. But if you soaked it long enough, then it wasn't so bad.

We started to walk together, and we saw Geoffrey there, sitting and swallowing his soup and bread down as if this was his last meal. Abner saw him and asked Goeffrey how's the soup? As he looked up, he noticed Abner and said, oh it's you what are you guys up to. Abner told him, just getting something to eat so I don't starve tonight. Then Abner said are these seats taken, and Geoffrey mumbled back with his mouth full of warm potato soup and said nay, help yourselves.

Geoffrey glanced at Cecil and thought, "Didn't you say yesterday you were using up your last ticket." I told him nay; I was just pulling your leg. As the three were drinking their soup someone, and it looked like Johnnie came running in past the doorman Benny and shouted to all of us, did you hear about the "Murder,' it happened down on O' Connell Street. They glanced up and when Johnnie blurted about a murder, most of them went back to eating their soup.

Benny asked Johnnie, when did you find this out. He said when he went down to Ha' Penny bridge that some were telling others about the story. So, Benny said, you overheard it. Yea, I guess, 'cause' I didn't see it.

Well thought Benny, he probably is making this up, so he can get his foot in the door and get a bowl of soup. Benny remembered the story Johnnie gave out to him and it was about a lady who was drowning in the Liffey River. And during that time of when he told it he had no tickets left, but he managed to get a bowl of soup. Benny just shook his head when he seen Johnnie on the line with a label and pouring him some soup in a bowl. He also managed to get a piece of stale bread.

Some of the bums were glancing around at others wondering how they were going to respond to this announcement. It seems they didn't know if they should believe Johnnie, or how to take the message that was blurted to them by someone who could make up stories. When Benny gathered his wits, he came up to Johnnie and asked, "Where on O'Connell Street" did they say the 'Murder' was committed? He said up there by the Liffey River down Eden Quay. I do not know exactly since I didn't want to go and see the scene of the crime. But I heard rumors that it was behind a Dive. Someone said it was probably something to do with money.

Johnnie was talking while still eating, hoping perhaps he could get seconds, and that Benny wouldn't notice. Of course, there was Margaret watching over the soup kitchen, for she helped prepare the homeless shelter. Margaret walked over to Benny and asked, "What is this I'm hearing. Is it really about a "Murder."

Benny assured her that she had not worry, it doesn't pertain to us. But then he gazed around and especially at Johnnie to see what he might do next. Cecil with the other two went over to talk to Johnnie to see if they could get the inside of this story. Cecil came up first with Geoffrey and Abner right behind, and Cecil said, hey man what gives about this 'Murder?' Johnnie looked at the three and said, "All I know is what I told Benny. I don't know much at all.

But sense you brought it up, there was one constable coming from the bar and saying to the other one that they had found some evidence. The other Irish constable gave him a whisper saying its about time we get a break on these cases.

I just happened to be standing close enough to hear and it seemed to them they didn't think much of me. I stood still not daring to move an inch. Abner glared at Johnnie saying weren't you scared at all. Johnnie said I was frightened to death. Are you kidding me. Cecil wonders where all this will lead too. His curiosity was getting the better of him, then he thought that none of this was any of his business.

Geoffrey said Well it's getting late and I'm heading back to my castle, as he started to roll his eyes, (seemly saying yea right.) His sense of humor was somewhat breath taking. We looked at him and said you're right. With a grin on our faces.

Starting out the door of the mission, Margaret and Benny told us to be careful out there. And they made an announcement to the hobos in the mission, saying make sure you guys get cleaned up and take a bath. You smell.

And they reminded us again be careful evidently there is some bad news, and it could lead to bigger problems than you realize.

As we went one by one, we all said our okays and byes in our own individual way. It seemed strange that we were going in three separate directions. Something I didn't seem to notice. Out of the four of us it was Cecil and Abner together, as Johnnie went in another direction and Geoffrey in another. Cecil asked Abner, have you ever been to Geoffrey or Johnnie place? Abner replied I've been at Geoffrey's, but I don't know where Johnnie stays.

Cecil inquires, where does Geoffrey stay? Abner in his shy way said in the direction you see him walking. Cecil looks at Abner, come on at least give me a general spot. Down towards Wellington Quay and then you take a left to an alley where an old, abandoned fishery house used to buy and sell fish from the mates that were on board a vessel. But that was before the war with United Kingdom in 1786. They finally gave us back Ireland in 1822, but we've had some issues. Starvation, jobs, and means to live,

Cecil was surprised of what Abner knew about Ireland's history. Cecil said, what are we going to do about it, Abner. He glandered hard into the sky and said it's beyond me. Then Abner considered talking about Irish history, what will become of us, Cecil. Cecil said honestly, I don't know but it doesn't look good. Besides the U.K. run everything. When they reached the spot that Abner called home, they lay down and stretched their legs then suddenly they both fell asleep.

*　　*　　*　　*　　*

When the sun came out and some noise was indicated down by Wellington Quay and the river, that's when Cecil woke up. He seen Abner has been up for a little while looking at his shoes. As Abner gazed at Cecil saying top of the morning to you Cecil; Cecil responded saying what are you doing Abner. 'Ah, it's me shoes,' they have seen better days. Cecil said to him, "What's wrong with your shoes? Abner said I've got a couple of holes in the sole, and I can feel them when I'm walking on pavement or rough ground.

As the two of them were sitting there looking at Abner's shoes, you could hear the stirring of cats as they were hunting for their breakfast. Between the rats, the mice, cats, and dogs there was always some form of movement.

Someone chasing someone. They would never mind you, but just stayed away from us, especially if we didn't want them around. Those scraggily dogs and cats probably never seen a bucket of water over them. Some even looked like they had lice or some form of scabies, for their hair would be matted up and even fallen out. I looked at Abner and asked him saying; aye Abner how long have we been living like this?

Abner glancing at me somewhat confused and replied saying, like what Cecil. I've been living like this since I was a wee-bit youngster still nursing from my mother. She had a hard time since Pop was always gone saying he was looking for the pot of gold that the leprechauns had left in Ireland. Mother would shout at him saying we need some better living conditions, mind you. And little Abner needs a father. He would shrug us both off with an excuse, at least that's what mother use to tell me when I was growing up, asking her, where's father and when he was coming back home.

She would say never mind your father he's a bum anyways. Then Abner just stared into the sky, knowing how bad his mother had it. Cecil listened and said I know what you're saying. We didn't have it any better either. He said it pains me at times how bad mother had it. It seems like she never got any help, from anybody but a few women folk she knew whom she grew up with.

They both sat there in silence thinking if only things could have been different. Now they are sitting around abandoned buildings, half torn up and falling apart from war and destruction. No means of making money except the fishing industrial, and a couple of factories with signs hanging out on their fences saying, "NOT HIRING," no work here.

Cecil asked Abner what he was going to do today, and Abner said he was going to go down on Wellington Quay. Cecil said you know you'll need a half-penny. Yea, I know said Abner. How are you going to get a half-penny? I don't know, but I'll think of something, he said. Abner glanced at Cecil and told him, "I'll see you later," maybe at the soup kitchen. Cecil mentions, okay maybe at the soup kitchen. Abner leaves tenderly knowing he has holes in the bottom of his shoes. And any kind of stone could hurt.

Cecil is thinking about going down to Middle Abbey Street to see if he could possibly make any money or earn some good food. He knows there are a few cooking shops. Some made bread, others had fish & chips, others had cafes.

He look upward and guessed it was close to 8:00 a.m. As Cecil was walking along, he was heading for Jervis Street, so he could see what was happening there. Besides it was a little detour to Middle Abbey Street. With nothing in his pockets, he was looking for anything that he could fill his gut with. Every now and then he would spot another hobo or moocher a bum just like him squandering his life away looking for grub to eat. For once Cecil couldn't believe how many beggars, loafers and spongers were wandering around for something to eat or steal. He knew there were quite a few, but all in one place or area. He decided to sit still at the corner of Jervis and

Great Strand Street and just watch all the activity running up and down the streets. There were some who had carriages as they were traveling from one place to another. Still others had wagons with 2-horses pulling them with certain products.

Well, it looked like nothing was around here, so I headed up Jervis Street and seen 'Fosters Grocery hut,' with hardly anything left but some ears of corn, potatoes, carrots, and greens for stew or cooking collard greens in a pot of onions and other scraps. I went up to Mr. Foster to ask how he was doing. Hi Cecil, was his reply, and he glanced at his products and said there isn't much here is there. But he said, Cecil grab a carrot if you want one. I stared at him and said thank you, Mr. Foster. I guess there is no reason for me to ask if you had some work that I could do to make a couple of pennies or perhaps a meal. No, I don't think so, look at my situation, Cecil I'm starting to go under. Cecil gazed at him very closely and said I'm sure it's not that bad. He glared with a long look, and he said, I don't know!

Cecil reassured Mr. Foster saying I hope things work out for you and your store. For you are one of the last ones who help the poor and needy. Foster smiled and laughed a little and he said, "I might be in the same boat" as you next week. Cecil walked off thinking, I hope Foster doesn't go under, he is one that I can count on. As Cecil walked up the street, he seen another merchant, and it was Mr. Howard with his business on the other side of the road.

While I walked up to Mr. Howard and said hello, I asked, how are you doing? He gasped and pondered about the question; things could be better was his remark. I knew he baked bread. His place was called 'Howard's Baking Factory.' He used to make donuts, cakes, bread of different sorts and even rolls and muffins. I looked at him and said what seems to be the problem.

And he looked disappointed at me and said, I don't have much money left to buy flour, sugar or other means to make bread. I only have a starter yeast to work with. My business is on the brink of going broke. I said surely, you're not that bad off. He emphasized I only have a week or two left if some sort of miracle doesn't happen. I told Mr. Howard before I left, good luck and hopefully things will start looking up.

When I reached Middle Abbey Street I looked off to the left. There were people going up and down the street and some kids running playing games. And when I turned my head and looked right there weren't too many people at all. So, I decided to go to the right. Maybe Mr. Asner can help me. Mr. Asner's sign read "ASNER'S BUTTER AND CREAM CHEESE," and the colors of that poor old sign was starting to fade away. If fact, you can barely read it. When I approached Mr. Asner I said, how's business? He shrugged his head in disappointment and said not too good. The cream and milk from the dairy cows are getting harder to find. So, that means the price increases also. We are just running into a stream of bad luck, was his comment.

I reluctantly said, I guess that means you can't hire me for something or even give me a small portion of some cheese. Not today young man, I just don't have any. Well thanks anyways Mr. Asner, we'll try some place else. He wished me good luck.

Well, I thought I'll still head in the same direction that I started and was getting close to Liffey Street. And when I stood on the corner, I looked in all directions wondering which way I would have some luck. It was well pass noon, probable closer to 3:00 p.m. I decided to sit and give it some thought. I was on the side of the road leaning my back up against the wall, pondering to myself, while sitting.

I could go down Liffey Street and that would make it closer to the soup kitchen, in which opened the line up at 6:00 p.m. Or go further down the road on Middle Abbey and come to O'Connell Street. There was usually more to offer on O'Connell than Liffey St. Besides I had 3- hours before soup time.

While I proceeded up Middle Abbey, I seen more boards and chains with locks on the front doors of establishments that went broke. The owners put these boards and locks with chains to keep bums like me out of there. They did this because there was too much vandalism and stealing of merchandise.

And the Constables didn't have a big enough force for all the criminalities that were going on in Dublin. While I proceeded up the street, I seen more Watering holes, Pubs, and Dives on one street then what I've seen in a while. That was about the same time I came across Chester, another poor broke bum, but in my opinion, he was a shyster. Like me he was feeding himself through charity and from the soup kitchens that were spread out in Dublin. I say to Chester, how's life been treating you? He saw me and said oh just fine Cecil, you finding anything, it seems everybody is starting to close their doors.

I told him yea; it appears they are going broke as we are. I looked at Chester and was asking him what soup kitchen he was going to. He told me that for the last couple of weeks he's been going to the one that was off Eden Quay, and it was on the corner of Beresford Place. I asked him how good the soup was there, and he said it was not very good, like eating hot water with some potato and onion flavor. He say you might get a chunk if you get lucky.

He asked me about the one I've been going to, and I told him about the same as you described. We determined that they are all about the same, when it comes to food. We got down about the middle of the street between Middle Abbey and Eden Quay on O'Connell and Chester said here's where I'm leaving you, so we'll see you. I just shook my head, and I thought good riddance Chester.

It appeared it was near 5:00 p.m. as I was walking toward Eden and I saw a woman approaching me as she was walking up O'Connell, and she went right pass me without a noise or any facial movement. Her stern face seem to give me all the answers that I might have had. She had a bonnet on her head and was wearing a light coat that was reaching below her knees. I turned around as she walked by me and asked if she would have the time. She said I don't own a watch of any sort of time piece, but the last time I saw it was 5:20. Then she turned back around and proceeded walking again.

As I turned to look towards Eden Quay, a wharf to speak of, when I haven't seen a fishermen's ship for years, anyways it was the U K taking most of our fish in their ships to feed the Brits and left us go hungry as usual. This was part of the history of Ireland. It appears the Brits got most of Ireland's resources, whether it was the fishery, iron ore, lumber, coal, and the lists go on. But Ireland at times manage to get enough to satisfy their countrymen in small doses. It was a horrible deal that Ireland got from the UK through the ages.

Maybe that is why we are like we are, starved and downtrodden people as we are. But there are a few left that are willing to fight, but it seems we are fighting each other just as bad as were fighting the Brits.

I gazed at the situation that Ireland and Dublin have fell into and it makes me wonder will we ever get out from all this atrocity. As I got out of this stupor, I realized about fifteen minutes have gone by.

Now I'm around the corner on Eden Quay and heading for the mission and it's before you get to Jervis Street. The place where I was last night. As I gander out at the water, Liffey River looks calmer than normal, and I see the pedestrians crossing Ha' Penny and each one stopping to pay their toll charge. As I went by the narrow bridge and getting closer to the small entry way leading to the road to the mission, I saw Abner standing there. It look as though he was waiting for someone or something.

When I got closer, he said how's it going Cecil? I told him I didn't find anything, but bad news. I glanced at him and said how about you. He replied it was about the same as it was yesterday. The stores are just getting poorer. And the owners don't know what to do and what's going to happen to them. When I gazed over to the river again, I mumbled to Abner, it doesn't look too good does it. He shook his head gently as his eyes glazed in the same direction I was looking at. When we thought let's walk up to the soup house and see about getting another free meal. Now this was Saturday and Benny opened the door for us beaten down bums to come in and see if we could get a bowl of soup that Margaret has prepared for the moochers who had no other place to go, but perhaps to another soup kitchen.

As Benny was standing at the door, he was letting some come in whoever had a ticket and suddenly standing at the door he seen the two of us. He looked at us with a smile and said, "Don't you remember what I said last night. As Abner looked at me frantically, I thought I would be honest. So, I told him, yea I remember.

Benny glared at me and said, "No odd or strange story tonight. My eyes sadden and heavy said, no sir I have nothing but my weary soul, standing here and begging for a bowl of soup. He glanced at me surprised and Margaret was standing behind him when I said it.

She shouted ah, gee-wiz get in here and get yourselves a bowl of soup.

Benny looked at her and said, why did you let that crumb in here? You know he's full of it. She embarked, yea I know but I didn't want to see if he would start crying. He said cry, he would of gave us another sympathy story.

As we were eating our soup there was better bread on a tray, so we all had a portion of it. About that time here came Johnnie running in and said wake up everybody, "there's been another Murder." Benny walked over this time and inquired to Johnnie, you say another "Murder," yea and the constables are getting scared, and some are angry about what happened. He asked Johnnie where's the murder at? He stopped for a moment thinking. Hmm. Between Benny and Margaret, they were getting somewhat anxious, and they implied, don't you know where you were!

The rest of us were questioning Johnnie saying, ah you didn't see or even hear about any murder. He shouted, yes, I did, now I know it was on O' Connell and down an alley behind a watering hole they called Lucky Lou's. Well, who did they find? I'm not sure they wouldn't let anybody go in the alley. But some snuck around and heard about some evidence that they had found. Yea when they had brought the body back out on a stretcher with a sheet over it, the others came back around and told us what the constables had to say. That's all I know.

Now the guys inside were buzzing about the possibilities and who the victim could have been, along with who the murderer might be. Benny along with Margaret had to keep them from insinuating and trying to solve a case that was all driven by speculation. It sure brought out the shock and disbelief that this has happened two-nights in a row, and it was close to home. For the watch showed on someone's wrist as it pointed to the 7 and 6 position. They asked Johnnie how long ago this occurred. He piped up thinking it was only 30- mins. Ago.

You mean they found the body at about 7:00 p.m. As Johnnie was filling his soup bowl and Benny was watching as he noticed it, and thought the little bugger is getting another meal without a ticket. Then he thought ah well, let him have it.

Margaret was standing there in awe, when the news came out about another murder. She spoke up saying who would do such a thing! Then one of the guys inside the soup kitchen mention about, the constables say they found some evidence. I wonder what it could be! And some looked at Johnnie while he was trying to eat his soup, and the annoyance of them just staring at him in the face, seem to get the better of him, finally Johnnie said don't look at me, I don't know.

Now the soup kitchen and the moochers and bums were sitting there wondering if going back home would be safe. As they were discussing this Benny and Margaret overheard their concern and offered, they could stay here an extra hour. So instead of leaving at 8:00 they could stay here until 9:00 p.m.

This had them wondering if it would be a good idea. I guess it didn't matter because it was still very dark outside. Some thought perhaps they should have left earlier, but they didn't hear the news until it was dark. You could see the look of worriedness and doubts announcing fear on their faces.

Then their thoughts became a little more relaxed as someone pointed out, what if we leave and go home in pairs. This way we have someone next to us that we could talk with. Margaret thought that would be an excellent idea, and Benny agreed wholeheartedly saying it's better than being alone. Well, the guys struck a deal and while they were discussing who was going with who was when two constables enter the room. Benny came over to them and asked is there something we could help you with?

One of the constables glanced at Benny and asked, "Are you the proprietor of this estate? And he answer back saying yes, I am. He looked with suspicion around the room as his partner was walking about and studying the hobos that were in there. And as he came up to me, he said where were you, at about 5:30 p.m. I told him walking down O' Connell Street. He said where abouts on O' Connell. I said, heading towards Eden Quay. And as he glanced at his partner, they both realized something. They looked attentively at my clothes, and said how long have you had tears in your coat? I told him that I've had some of these tears for a couple of years.

He and his partner said we would like to take you down at the station so you can answer some questions relating on your whereabouts. So, I asked what have I done? They said nothing yet. But we are just going through the process. I gazed at all the people in the mission. Margaret came to my defense and inquired I've known Cecil for a long time, now I'm asking what this, is all about, and what has he done to have you take him down to the station?

And out of the corner of my eye I seen Benny approaching the constable that Margaret is engaged with. The other constable was keeping an eye on everyone else that either was sitting or standing there with a blank face showing doubtfulness.

While they were questioning the accusations, the constables were within their jurisdiction, and they kept reassuring Margaret and Benny, if he's innocent then he should have no problems. Then Margaret was observant enough to ask why did you keep looking at his coat and picked him out instead of anyone else? This, is just a typical informal procedure that we go through so we can exclude him if he shows he's innocent.

But Margaret was persistent saying, why did you keep looking at him, as if he could be guilty of something. And she kept asking, what are you questioning him about, that you must take him down to the station? But the constables would not relate to them what they would be questioning him about. Both Margaret and Benny glared at the constables, wondering if this is within the law, taking someone down to the station and not tell them the reason why, or what the questions would be about. When the constables kept reassuring them this is a routine procedure, finally Margaret and Benny stood there in awe and was silent. When Margaret with Benny looked at both constables, they seemed to be just doing their jobs. As Margaret stepped over to me with sympathy in her eyes, Benny followed by shaking his head in somewhat disbelief that this was happening. I was standing near Abner and Benny asked me in a shush way if I was innocent of any wrong doings. I told them I didn't do anything wrong that I know of. And they both believed me along with Abner who was standing close enough to hear the conversation.

Finally, when the situation was stable the two constables came over and one of them put cuffs on me. "Margaret said "do you have to do that with irritation on her face. He said its standard procedure mam. She shook her head and said we'll help you as best as we can. I told her don't worry that I should be back in no time.

*   *   *   *   *

While the two constables assisted me on the back of the wagon, they rode on the benches of this newer buckboard style wagon. I asked one of them where we were going. He said, down at the station. I said yes, I know that but where? He said our zone is in Pearse Street, Garda station. How far is that I asked. The one who had the reins to the horse said it was about 1-1/2 or 2- miles from here.

I thought and asked what type of questions, are they going to ask me. Oh, said the one just sitting there casual like and said things like where were you at such and such time. Who have you talked to. What have you been doing on certain days; you know things like that. Okay was my response. As we were riding in the dark there were some kerosene lanterns on at corners and a few during long straight-aways. It seem they had one every 250 ft. all along the Quay's.

As we were crossing O'Connell bridge, it seem rather odd to me that I haven't been down this way in a long time. It seem the scenery was different from what I remember. After crossing the bridge, we came up to Burgh Quay and when we crossed it, we were on D'Oiler Street. As we traveled a little further, there was an intersection that connected six- different roads. And straight ahead off to the left there was a sign that said Pearse Street Garda Station.

When the constables pulled up to the side of the entry way, one assisted me off and said follow me. The other one opened the door and after we walked in the other said stand still and I'll take these cuffs off. Then he escorted me to a wooden bench along the corner of a room and said wait we'll be with you in a minute.

When the two- constables came back they brought someone with them, and he was carrying a rather large envelope with him. As he approached, he offered a handout so he could give me a handshake. I got up off the bench and held my hand out to his response. He introduced himself and said I'm District Inspector 2nd class Harry Byrnes, now who may I be talking to? I told him I'm Cecil Offlay. He introduced the two constables who brought me in as Constable Geoff and Henry. He said have a seat this, may take a while.

He put his left hand on his chin and kind of rubbed it slightly as he was looking away and said, "I have something in my right hand inside this envelope that may startle you. I looked at him oddly as my head slightly cocked to the side wondering what he may have in that package, he calls an envelope. As he hesitated, he said is there anything you want to tell me about the last two days.

I looked at him rather profoundly and said what is it you want to know. He walked around in small circles examining my emotions and reaction as I was just sitting there wondering what he was trying to get to. As he reached for his head and started scratching it, he didn't seem to get a response from my action. Rather he looked as if he was getting somewhat puzzled from my non-chalant attitude.

Now I could tell he was getting a little frustrated from our interaction and I asked, why did you guys bring me here. They looked at me and said one moment we what to have a little conference within our department and we'll be right back. But in the meantime, can we borrow your coat. Cecil asked, "What do you want with my coat. Cecil had been told that they would like to see if it matches something they'd been working on. I inquired what are you working on? One of them said it's the color that intrigues us and we would like to see if we can match it. Cecil said the color! One of them said yea it's the color.

Earlier they sent for a man and his wife, both were (professional expert on clothing material,) and had him and her come in with the escort of an Acting Constable 2nd class. And when they finally returned was about the same time, they retrieved Cecil's coat. Now when they handed over the envelope to Adrian and Clara, they opened the package and each one felt and looked at the fabric and texture and to see if it was woven, knitted, or a fibrous material. They were checking the smoothness of the cloth. As they both were discussing the material out loud the Inspector reminded them that he could here you and we are in a station.

When the comparison was finished, they both determined this make was of the same woven cloth. They said this cloth is common. They asked about the color. Now this is where the answer got somewhat surprising. They said about two years back they quit making this color. The constables asked why. The professionals said they had a hard time selling this color. So, they quit making them. They looked at the three and said is there anything else Inspector. He said no, I just don't know how I will proceed in this case. But he did say to Adrian and Clara if needed would you make this same statement in court? They responded with a yes.

The inspector turned to Acting Constable 2 and told him that he could take Adrian and his wife back when they are ready. If you find anything else about the material, please let me know. They nodded their heads in agreement.

The two Constables looked at the Inspector and said what are you going to do? He said I have a few more questions for Cecil. Inspector asked one of the constables to come with him and directed the other to look at your next assignment and Henry went with him after Geoff talked it over, saying you spotted my man, so you should go with the Inspector.

So, Henry went with the Inspector, and he told the constable to follow his lead. Henry nodded his head with a concern understanding. As they approached Cecil the Inspector gave him his coat as he said I have a series of questions for you Cecil before I can let you walk through those doors. While he said that Cecil laid his coat on the wooden bench he was sitting on.

First said the Inspector, where were you tonight at about 4:00 p.m. and please give me all the details up until you entered the mission. He began by saying as I was walking on Abbey Street I went over to Asner's Butter & Cream Cheese, and that was probably a little after 4:00 say about 4:15. And I asked him if he needed any help, because I'm trying to make a little money or perhaps get some cheese. Asner told me that business wasn't doing very well, and the price of milk and cream has increased and that he's on the verge of going belly up.

Then I proceeded up Abbey Street and I come to the corner of O'Connell and Abbey, and I took a right going towards Eden Quay's. I say it was probably about 5:00 as I was going down the street and I didn't see anything but some wagons going through and there seemed to be light loads on them. Then about 5:25 I was at the other corner and looked out at the river and I stood there wondering or perhaps dreaming, have I ever seen times that was pleasant.

Then about 5:45 I went along the Quay and headed to Benny's and Margaret mission to see about getting a bowl of soup and then I ran into Abner. We talked before we entered. That's all I've done since that time.

The Inspector said is there anything else, I mean did you forget anything. Then he brought it up, asking, what did you do at the Quay. Cecil looked at him, what Quay? He said when you were down there at Eden Quay, and you were looking or dreaming at the river. Cecil thought and said I don't really recollect what I was thinking about. Accept the things that the Brits have done to us.

Then the Inspector told the Constable to have Geoff go down to the morgue and see if they can identify where they were from. If they are from the UK, we could have a motive. So go quick, I'll be waiting.

As the Inspector reached to his coat and looked at it very closely, he said to Cecil, you have a lot of pieces missing on the outer layer of your coat. What happened to your coat? Cecil glanced at the Inspector and said pieces just seem to fly off as if it was starting to rot away.

Then Cecil asked the Inspector, why am I here, and what do you suspect from me. He took a hard look into my eyes and said, "What do you think? I pondered on that. I guess I'm here about what has happened the last two nights, but I say I don't know anything about them. Cecil looked so sincere to the Inspector that his first thought was he may be telling the truth. Then he thought may be this man his so crafty that he can lie with out any remorse, (such as a serial killer.) or perhaps a mental delusionist that doesn't seem to remember his actions.

As the Inspectors mind kept rolling around in his head about a half-hour has rolled by. Then Constable Henry came back with some vital information, whispering in the ear of the Inspector stating that the two victims were indeed Brits. Then he paused and was thinking how to approach the perpetrator. Now suddenly Cecil is considered a perp. As the Inspector was thinking, he approached Cecil with a bit of concern saying, now Cecil have you left out anything. I mean anything, such as meeting people or talking with anybody on O'Connell Street. He said take your time and think very hard before you answer me, okay.

Cecil glanced at the Inspector and towards the Constable, wondering what do they want from me. He sat there with a Hmm. On his face. Then he said I did me a couple of people on that street. The Inspector asked him who did you meet first. He said I came up to Chester. The Inspector asked where on O'Connell did you see Chester? Cecil thought about it carefully and eventually said I ran into him as we were going down O'Connell towards Eden and about half-way down the road, he told me that he had to leave, and he went across the street on O'Connell and that was the last time I seen him.

The Inspector asked, what did you two talk about? Cecil said not much, but we did talk about the missions we were going to. So, he asked me what mission is Chester going too? Well, he told me the one down there on the corner of Beresford Place and Eden Quay. He asked me what time was that? I told him probably about 5:15p.m. because I stopped a lady later and asked her if she knew the time. She told me she didn't have a timepiece but said earlier she seen a clock that said 5:30p.m. and we both turned around and went our separate ways.

Why did you stop the lady for. I looked at him and said I just told you, to see what time it was because the doors open up at 6:00p.m. at Benny's mission.

The Inspector notice it was getting late and he took his timepiece out from his vest, and it showed it was 11:30 at night and then he said to me. You wouldn't mind spending the night here with two of our Constables, would you? He went further as I gave him a rather odd facial expression, asking him am I under arrest. He said no it's not that, but it will save us and you a trip back to Osmond Quay. Besides we have some nice cots here and you're welcomed to one.

The Inspector seemed to be a cordial fellow and I had this weird feeling that I could trust him. So, I asked which one shall I take, because I'm getting tired. He had his Constable lead me to an empty cell at the end of the hall and he said good night as he left. I laid down for the first time in months on a comfortable mat with a blanket and pillow.

As the morning swiftly went by the Constable came up to me with something on a plate. He asked if I wanted some breakfast. There was an unexplainable shock that set upon my face when he said, 'would you like to have some breakfast.' I don't remember when I had a breakfast. I said to him thanks and he handed me the plate. When I looked at the plate, I saw a fresh egg scrambled up, with potato hash, a piece of fat back and a slice of bread. I gazed at that and thought I went to heaven. And before he left, I said thank you again.

The Constable looked back and said there is a washroom on the other side of the hall, and you're welcomed to use it. I nodded my head up and down for my mouth was full at the time. When I finished the plate, I sat there satisfied looking at myself wondering if I needed to get cleaned up. Because it being a week, I thought it would be wise to use the washroom while I had a chance.

Constable Henry came in just when I was finished in the washroom and said to me how is your morning. I said it's been nice. He said I came back here so you could talk to District Inspector 2nd class, for he wants to see you. I took a quick glance at Henry and then I said what for. Well, you know how Inspectors are, they don't ever seem to be satisfied with someone's answers.

As we walk to another room, he was waiting for me. To where I found out this is his office. He glared at me and said good morning, Cecil I trust you had a good stay here. I question the Inspector with the Constable saying, I noticed my coat was missing is there a reason why?

Yes we put it in our coat closet, where we keep coats at, so it doesn't have to lie on the floor. Oh, I thought, okay. I looked at both of them and said when will you let me go back home. That's when the

Inspector piped up and said, well Cecil we still have some questions that we need answers too. As I pondered for a couple of minutes I said, "that sounds like I'm being arrested. And the Inspector was quickly to say, 'ah no, no,' you are merely here as a witness for questioning.

I began to now wonder who is being played as a sucker. But I reminded them that I have nothing else to tell. And the Inspector studied my reasoning and said sure you do. He said we went over where and who you seen yesterday, but we didn't go over what you did the day and night before. He inquired to me don't you recall.

But I said that doesn't have anything to do with what happened last night. Does it! The Inspector said I believe it does. You see we found evidence from both scenes, and they are alike. So, we had two murders in two nights, or should we say early evening around 6:00 p.m. and we have the same evidence from both scenes. You see my dilemma, and do you see where I'm coming from. Is it a coincidence or not. I say it isn't said the Inspector. I believe somebody murdered the two victims wearing the same coat and they accidentally left a piece of it behind.

I was amazed at his deduction. And so was the Constable. So, he said with a long sigh, and that's when he looked at me. Okay Cecil let's go over what you did the day before. He said let's begin at about 3 or 4:00 p.m. and tell me everything.

I asked the Inspector to let me think about it for a few minutes, because the day was a little fuzzy. The Inspector said while you're thinking about that I'll be back in a few moments. Inspector and Constable Henry went over to the corner of the room and was talking low enough to where I couldn't hear them.

The inspector was asking if Constable Geoff was on the assignment of tracking this Chester character. And Henry told him that he went to the mission and found out he was there last night having soup, but then left about 7:00 p.m. last night. So, he still hasn't found him but he's looking. And Geoff, by Cecil's description is telling their Constables to keep an eye out for him. And if someone spots him to get word back to him. And he also gave word that this is something the Inspector needs, and he wants it badly, he said because of heat up the line.

Well sir I believe they are keeping an eye out diligently. I hope so he said sternly. The Constable was starting to sense frustration coming from the Inspector, but he knew he was a patient man. But if he got enough heat upstairs then his temperament would start to dwindle.

When District Inspector 2nd Class Harry Byrnes came up to me he seemed rather focused very intently on my answers. The first question that came out of the Inspector's mouth was, tell me where you were and what you were doing at 4:00 p.m. two- days back. Cecil said to the best of my knowledge I was on Middle Abbey Street and walking slowly towards O'Connell Street. Then the Inspector looked attentively at my answer and said okay Cecil; Did you see anybody or stop anywhere? As I studied the question I said yes I did.

He stared at me and said where was that and who was it. I told him that I walked into Waldo's Public House and sat there for a few moments. Then what said the Inspector. Well, I went up to the bar and asked Waldo if I could get a glass of water. So, what did Waldo say. He said to wash my throat down someplace else or order an ale. Then I asked him what would be the harm to wash my throat down with water. And the people in the Pub was getting loud and they were laughing and shouting. I saw Waldo was starting to get mad, so I started to leave, and they called me a scallywag on the way out. The Inspector asked me, "do you know what the time was then?" I said it must have been about 5:00 p.m.

After that I left, thinking I didn't want to go back home yet so I started walking heading for the soup kitchen. Okay, what did you do as you're walking on O'Connell Street. Oh, nothing much, just walking towards Eden and Ormond Quay. Did you have the same coat on then as you do now. Yes I wear it everywhere, so I don't lose it.

Inspector continued, did you see or stop anyplace else before you got to the soup kitchen. Yea, I did, I saw Abner on Ormond Quay heading for the mission too. And we stopped and was talking about the day. The inspector asked what did you guys talk about. Well, he told me that he was down there on Lower Ormond Quay and even the fishermen didn't have anything. Abner said it appears there's nothing around. And I told him about Waldo's Place and what happened there, and that I didn't find much of anything there either.

When the Inspector got his story from Cecil, he inquired to Constable Henry to put Cecil back in the cell to wait. Cecil turns to the Inspector and said when are you going to let me go? The inspector looks at Cecil and says after I look at all of the evidence, then I'll make a recommendation to the Deputy Inspector General. As we were walking back to the cell I said to the Constable, they are never going to let me go, are they. He will find something to arrest me on, won't he?

Constable Henry didn't say a word but glanced at Cecil with worriedness. He told Cecil that he will be back to see him later. That is when he heard the door lock behind him. It was 10:15 a.m., and Cecil finds himself stuck in a cell with nothing to do but think and worry about what just happened and what could happen next. He decided to lie on the cot and stare at the ceiling that needed fixing.

Cecil heard footsteps coming and it was another Constable. He had a plate and sat it down on a short, small stool. He brought the stool next to the bars and told me to go back and put my hands on the wall. He said that's if you want to get fed. So, I did as ordered, and he unlocked the door and brought the stool in and left it. He said I hope you enjoy your dinner. I asked him, where's Henry at? He told me he's on assignment. As I put the stool by my cot, I sat and ate a good meal. It was pork with two slices of bread and water.

It seemed as though the whole afternoon went by before I seen anybody. And it was the Inspector along with the two Constables that I met before. While the one Constable opened the cell door he said come out Cecil, we have some questions for you. They led me back to the Inspectors office and they closed the door behind them.

The inspector turned to me and said, while I talked to the District Inspector General that we came up to the conclusion that we will have to hold you. I glared at him and said on what charge are you holding me on? He seemed to be reluctant on the words of using suspicious suspect. I glanced at the two Constables Henry and Geoff wondering what that actually means. As I nodded curiously I stated to them what makes me a suspect? The Inspector says well you have the material of your coat left at the crime scene and on both evenings you were close to the murders at about the same time.

I said that seems odd for there were other people around too. But they don't have a coat like you do.

So, Cecil you are the only suspect we have. Until we find out it's someone else you're the one who is on top of the list. That is why we are keeping you in custody. I do have some promising news, and that is these two Constables believe of your innocence. And they want to help you. As I shook my head up and down I said I'm glad someone believes me. Now the Inspector said I'm going to leave you three alone, because I have other issues that I need to attend to. Cecil before I leave, you do know the consequences, right? Yes I think so, Inspector, and thank you. The Inspector shook his head sideways as he was leaving.

So, I asked the two Constables where do we start. The one said first Cecil call us Henry and Geoff, so we don't get mixed up. Okay came out of my mouth. Geoff asked me saying I've been trying to locate Chester, but we've been having a hard time, and we wonder is there anybody else who knows Chester, or does he have any friends that could help us out in finding Chester. Cecil thought about it but couldn't remember anybody that knew him in the slightest. Then I asked Geoff why did he want to know.

He said the notes he got from Henry state that you ran into Chester before the second murder, and he crossed the street on O'Connell on the same side as Eden Quay and perhaps he went down pass Eden Quay towards the mission that he goes too. And you also said it was pass 5:00 p.m. Because you ran into this woman and asked her the time and she said it was about 5:20 p.m. before you stared at Liffey River and then you said you went on Ormond Quay towards the mission that you go to.

Cecil peered at Geoff and said yea, that sounds about right. So, Geoff said that's why we need to find Chester. For he's your only hope that I see. Hmm. I got to thinking that I heard someone say they knew something about Chester. When I heard silence for a few minutes, I popped up from where I was sitting and told them about Abner. He told me something about Chester, because when we were talking about him I asked "do you know where he stays' and have you ever been there. He told me he was at one of his places, he said that

Chester told him that he had two places. You need to talk to Abner, and you can find him at the mission eating soup from 6:00 p.m. to 8:00 p.m. they close the doors after that.

After Geoff and Henry had a few more questions that they escorted me back to my cell. Now it was 6:00 and my supper tray came in. We went through our routine and when I looked at the plate, I seen a slice of ham with a small potato beside it and a couple of cooked carrots.

When the second night passed by; the morning was here and the first thing I saw was the man saying do you need to use the washroom. I told him yes the one outside, for you guys have been feeding me well. The constable had me put my hands through the bars and put one cuff on my wrist and then he said take your hands out and put the other cuff on the other wrist. Then he opened the door cell and had me walk in front of him heading for the outside door.

I thought to myself, is this what they called house arrest last night when I heard them over talking about me. I guess so, it appears anytime I'm released from that cell that I have cuffs on. I even have cuffs on when I'm in the washroom. As day had passed the evening was starting. The two constables Henry and Geoff came by to visit me for a few minutes, and they told me they haven't had any luck yet. Abner says that he doesn't remember but we are working on him, and Benny with Margaret ask if they could come by to visit. And I told him them it would be alright. But Geoff and I are working on a plan, Geoff is taking and watching the mission on Beresford Place and I'm sticking by Abner.

We should luckily find something out soon, but in the meantime you'll have to stay here. Cecil said to them, thanks for believing in me. They shook their heads and said their goodbyes. The night went by slowly until I fell asleep. Then the morning showed up and it seemed that it was almost a repeat from yesterday. So, the third night passed by without any new information. I washed up and had a small breakfast, but I didn't have any visitors.

It was about 1:00 p.m. when Benny and Margaret appeared in front of me after I had a soup with real potatoes and onions with a bread roll. They asked me how I was doing. I said for the most part, okay. Benny told me do you realize the charge they have against you. Yea, I think its what they call house arrest or perhaps suspicious suspect. Benny took a rather hard gander at me and said it's called "Murder. "Cecil don't you realize they have you on being the main suspect in "Murder!"

Yea, I suspect I knew that too, but I couldn't believe it. Why do you believe or know that Cecil. Margaret also made me aware that if they don't find the murderer then you will be him and your goose will be cooked. They said they had to leave and prepare soup for the day. But before they left, I told them you need to get a hold of Abner, because he knows something about where Chester might live.

They had a somewhat quizzical look on their faces and thought what does Chester have to do with this.

Cecil just told him that the Inspector wants to talk to him. but they can't find him. Okay Cecil we'll talk to Abner and see what gives. I appreciate it guys and thanks for coming to see me. They left with a hidden frown on their faces, as if I was already doomed.

The evening came with supper then the night approached, and I was asleep again. There was no more visitors accept the constable that took me to the outhouse. The morning sun rose as the constable came by to bring a plate for breakfast then he left me without a message. While the fifth day came I had a visit from the Inspector saying that the 'District Inspector General' with the approval of the "Inspector General has charged you with 'Murder'!"

Sorry to tell you this Cecil, but your time is running out. There will be counsel to see you tomorrow and he will go over your case. He will introduce himself tomorrow. But let's wait to see what Constable Henry and Geoff come up with.

I'll leave you with your thoughts Cecil. I'm sorry about the bad news. It was finally hitting me about the situation that I happen to be in. Oh my, was something that I was thinking about, then the penalty of murder is hanging the accused. Now I was being accused. I laid there in bed waiting on more bad news. It was like it was coming in droves. There was a mental picture that just happen to appear. It was me standing there at the hangman's noose on a platform for everyone to see. I dreaded that picture when I seen people there that I've known.

Supper was brought to me and the constable that served me didn't say a word, he just had a plate of food waiting for me to back up and touch the wall as usual. And when the cell door was locked again he looked at me as if he seen a murderer. I was somewhat puzzled about his reaction. After supper I just laid there waiting to see if anybody will visit me.

Constable Geoff and Henry came by and there seemed to be a disappointment in their eyes. They kind of shook their head saying we haven't found anything yet. I asked; How about Abner hasn't he say anything or show you where he could possibly live? He just says he can't remember. Has Benny and Margaret talk to him. Yes they have. There're doing all they can, now Cecil started getting a little emotional saying they are going to try me in court.

Yea, we know Cecil. Geoff spoke up saying is there any other missions that Chester would go to? Cecil stared in the air looking at the walls, he said I don't know of any other. Have you talk to the guys at that mission. No, we haven't they ignore us, either scared or maybe they think they might get into trouble. I told them yea, I know what they mean, look at me.

Cecil gave them an idea saying I would present myself and walk up as a hobo and ask them if anybody has seen Chester. And when they ask what do you want with him. You say he's a friend and he told me if I ever got this way to ask for him. See what happens, because I'm getting desperate. Geoff got to thinking maybe tomorrow night I could get one of the sub or acting constables to go undercover. Henry glanced at him are you kidding. No, we could tell them they are on an important case and if they can help solve this case they could be in line for a promotion. Henry laughed about the suggestion. Then he says...

Sounds good, said Henry, "were open to any suggestions. Well, we got to go Cecil and hang in there. Now that wasn't a funny joke, Geoff. Oh, I'm sorry I didn't mean it that way. Eventually Cecil falls asleep with the worries he has and was just dead tired of the whole ordeal.

Next morning, he goes through the same typical routine and is sitting in his cell when the legal counselor was standing at the cell door. He introduced himself as Dublin's Legal Counsel of Dublin District 2. His name Edgar Winston Jr. . It was probably about 10:00 in the morning when he was talking to the counselor.

As the counsel went over the same trivial things as I had done with the Inspector, he told me that we'll have a hearing or perhaps a trial in two days. He said it was undecided, it depends on the evidence. As he collected his notes, he told me he will be here tomorrow around the same time. And he said if you find some new evidence that will help your case, let me know.

I said goodbye counsel and that I will see you tomorrow. The rest of the day I just moseyed along trying to remember any details that might stick out. Later, after I had my supper it felt like a couple of hours went bye so I asked a constable by shouting out through the bars if he could tell me the time. He told me quit shouting, what do you want said the constable. I wanted to know what time it is and if I'll see anybody. He announced that it said 8 bells on the clock.

I told him thanks and I didn't mean to shout. He said forget it I won't see you much longer. And he started to walk away.

Now frustration has entered my train of thoughts. I thought maybe I would of heard something by now. After an original introduction the constables came by and told me they are using my suggestion about the undercover hobo, but nothing has occurred from it. But the individual is still acting as a hobo, and we'll see if we can get to Chester. Margaret seems to think that Abner is finally getting the picture on what is truly happening, because he asks for you.

Cecil looked at them and said I've only got tomorrow before they put me before a judge in a courtroom. At least that is what my Legal counsel said. I don't know how I'm going to get out of this. I guess you guys are doing the best you can. Now Geoff and Henry were kind of dazing at the wall and ceiling, not knowing what to say.

But Geoff said we still have a day and a night left. Hopefully something will turn up tomorrow. Well, good night Cecil I got to go, and Henry was right behind him saying keep your faith.

When they left it put Cecil in a despondent feeling, feeling sad about what's happening. He lasted until after midnight and finally fell asleep. Tiredness has overcome him.

The next morning came with a sound of silence, and he wondered where everybody was at. A few moments went by, and a constable came by with his breakfast, so he went through the same routine once again.

When he was through with his breakfast he hoped that this could be a better day. He suddenly heard the Legal Counsel at the jail room door. As he entered the constable was standing beyond talking sounds and was there for the counsel's protection.

We went through the same ordeal to make sure he address it properly. Then he asked if there was anything to add, and I said no sir, not at this time. He reminded me the court date was tomorrow at 10:00 a.m. I told him I was aware of the court date and time. He said I'm giving you a warning this case is kind of flimsy if we have nothing else. I responded by saying yes I know.

Well, I went through the day with the same process of what I did yesterday. I had some time to think, had meals at their proper times, had no visitors when the counsel had left. Everything seem to stay the same, but when darkness approached was the time that Geoff and Henry came by with some news, saying that there undercover man has spotted Chester and has been following him.

He found his home and he told another constable to tell us. So, we are in route to find his home and see what he has to say. We will bring him in and start questioning him. We got to go but try postponing the trial saying some new evidence has been found.

When the time came they put cuffs on me again and when the Legal Counsel and a few constables showed up they stuck me on the back of the wagon and put another set of cuffs from the cuffs I had to the fence rail of the wagon. I told my counsel about some new evidence coming and it seems he was just ignoring my latest report. I requested he would postpone this trial until the new evidence has been looked at. He was perplexed about my opinion about how to run a legal system. He told me we will need to address the judge and the court for your granting of a postponement. It's not I who makes up the rules.

We were heading to Dolphin Court off of Essex Street and Sycamore Street. This court was in the District. I asked my counsel who was presiding as Judge. My counsel looked at me rather oddly and said does it make a difference? I said it could. He said how's that. I said some are more lenient than others. He mumbled yes that's possible. It was 9:00 a.m. as we entered through the front doors with cuffs wrapped around my wrists as the so- called audience stared with awe on their faces. I could hear whispering under their tongues as I heard some say is that him. When things seemed to get settle down some it was 9:35a.m. showing on the big grandaddy clock.

Now we took our seats the counsel goes over his speech, and I sat there wondering what kind of sentence will they(the court) give me, as punishment for "MURDER." As the trial began the prosecutor was making a case of why he(meaning me) needs the death sentence. He kept on insinuating of why I should be denounce and given the death sentence. My counsel just kept sitting there without to much objection or fighting back as a Legal Counsel. I asked my counsel when will you ask for a postponement for we I mean the constables have found new evidence.

He told me to never mind we have it all under control. Now it was 10:35 a.m. and I could tell this court has made up its mind. I was heading for the gallows. The people haven't seen a hanging since 23 I'd say a little over 2- year ago. I just shook my head and looked around and I was paying attention to what the judge was doing. His fingers seemed like they were getting itchy for the gavel.

About the time when I thought everyone had their decision made up about sending me to the gallows, the judge reached for his gavel before the doors opened up and you could hear shouting from two constables with an Inspector saying stop the trial. We have found the guilty party and he's locked up in our cell.

We have found the perpetrator and evidence and there was criminality on his part. Besides, he pled guilty on all charges.

Now the court system went berserk when they were willing to let an innocent man to hang for bad judgement and laziness on their part. There was some questioning from higher ups about the legal system that we call the Law.

Cecil was released on the courts step, and he told the constables and all that helped him thank you for giving me my Freedom back.

After that Cecil had some friends, but most of the audience in the courthouse were still in shock, he paused and thought for now I'm an innocent man.

Milton Keynes UK
Ingram Content Group UK Ltd.
UKHW022038301123
433552UK00016B/846